BE HERE
TO LOVE ME
AT THE
END OF THE
WORLD

BE HERE
TO LOVE ME
AT THE
END OF THE
WORLD

SASHA FLETCHER

MELVILLE HOUSE
BROOKLYN · LONDON

BE HERE TO LOVE ME AT THE END OF THE WORLD

First published in 2022 by Melville House
Copyright © Alexander Fletcher, 2021
All rights reserved
First Melville House Printing: February 2022

Melville House Publishing
46 John Street
Brooklyn, NY 11201
and
Melville House UK
16/18 Woodford Road
London E7 0HA

mhpbooks.com
@melvillehouse

ISBN: 978-1-61219-947-4
ISBN: 978-1-61219-948-1 (eBook)

Library of Congress Control Number: 2021947524

Designed by Beste M. Doğan

Cover image by Stefano Politi Markovina / Alamy Stock Photo

Printed in the United States of America
1 3 5 7 9 10 8 6 4 2

A catalog record for this book is available from the Library of Congress

For Alex, for this broken nation, and for everyone who has ever loved.

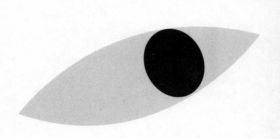

**A LOVE STORY
IN A BAD DREAM
ABOUT AMERICA.**

IT'S BROOKLYN. It's winter. It's so cold outside that you could execute billionaires in the street and it hasn't even snowed. In the aisles of the supermarket, the landlords gather. The sun has gone down and all around is darkness. It is 4:30 at night on a Sunday afternoon. People've wrapped the bare and shaking trees that line the streets in Christmas lights. It's almost beautiful. Sam and Eleanor are sitting in a bar. Later, Eleanor'll ask him to tell her a story. Later, tanks will roll through the streets. The sky will look like you've never seen it before. It'll look like a movie. It'll change your life. Then there'll be a history lesson, followed by a reasonably good dinner, but after that, it's the end of the world.

Meanwhile, Eleanor and Sam are in love, they live together and everything, and it's been a long week of missed deadlines and unread invoices and, as I mentioned, no snow, so they went out for a drink and, wouldn't you know it!, the moment Sam walked into the bar at 4:30 at night on a Sunday afternoon, snow fell, hip high, from the sky, and it just kept falling and falling and falling until, one day, far in the distant future, it stopped. Eleanor was already at the bar, waiting for him. She went out to look for a book she really wanted, about all the different times the world ended due to total disaster and ecological collapse, and Sam had some emails to send regarding invoices. I should let you know that Sam had maybe three or four outstanding invoices that would each cover rent for a month but not one of them had been paid yet, it really looked, according to the software Sam had installed to see if his emails had been opened, like those emails he had sent were just sitting there, unopened, and this caused Sam a good deal of distress, to know that he could easily make rent and maybe even take Eleanor out for dinner if people would just pay him the money they owed him for the work they'd contracted him to do, but they had not yet done this, and it gave Sam a very bad feeling inside. Not having money is a very very bad feeling to have, and I hope you never have to have it. As Sam opens the door to the bar his glasses fog up, he can't see a single thing, and he realizes, in this moment, that maybe what he should do is not put INVOICE as the subject, and instead he should act as though he was about to do some free work for them, and then they open the promised sample, and look, it is not a sample at all, but an invoice!, and proof that it has been seen! This is a good plan, to scam his way into being paid for the work he has done, he thinks, as Eleanor says, "Sam!" and he smiles with his whole face. Today, in New York City, the cops shot fifteen unarmed people, and two armed people.

So now, for the first time all winter, it's snowing.

Outside, the snow is now falling with such heaviness it sets off car alarms, which are then muffled by the weight and depth of the snow covering the cars like a blanket or a body or the end of the movie. Sam takes his fogged-up glasses off, and he looks around, and he blinks as Eleanor takes his hand and he sits down beside her.

So now Sam and Eleanor are sitting at the bar while outside the snow falls and falls, they're talking about how, while

Sam was walking over to the bar with his phone in his pants under his parka, where he could not reach it to see, the President told everyone that it was possible a nuclear missile was going to hit New York. Everyone in the bar is talking about it and Sam just wants a drink.

It's a hundred years later, the clouds are gone, everything's on fire, and the air's fucked. For the next hundred years, hurricanes the size of Texas rip across the continent, spitting up the boiling ocean and the rotting husks of everything that ever died all over your lawns. A thousand years later, birds show up. They grow bigger and bigger and bigger. Ten thousand years later their wingspans are the size of houses. They tear at the earth, and they eat up your dreams, and they weep. You can track the promises we made to each other each time we crawled out of the sea whenever you look to the sky. Next time will be so different.

Sam and Eleanor are walking home from the bar. It is freezing! Eleanor burrows into him for warmth. "I will wear your skin like a hot wet blanket to save me from this weather!" she says to him, "Baby, I will carry you with me for all of my days." They make it home to their rent-stabilized two-bedroom in Crown Heights, where the second bedroom is big enough for a very small child (who can't even pay rent, the child, any child!, because in 1938 America passed the Fair Labor Standards Act, which restricted children under sixteen from working in manufacturing and mining, and in 1941 it was mandated as constitutional by the Supreme Court, and anyway the quote unquote second bedroom is absolutely too small for a sixteen-year-old, but it's great for an office), and they take off all their clothes and they crawl, together, naked, into bed.

The streetlights come on. The snow is falling so heavy that all you can see is the snow, and the lights, and the night.

As the city sleeps, the subways begin their slow march towards service failure. Everyone in New York City dreams about a nuclear missile turning the sky green, and screaming. They dream about new civilizations, a wholly new humanity composed of pure thought winding their way to the heavens from the subway tunnels where their dreams were born, they dream of Yankee Stadium's last stand, the final slugger, stepping up to knock the nuke out of the park and into the sun, the final grave, they dream, they scream, in their dreams, they cry. I'm sorry to be the one to tell you this. Take a sip of water, please, and just close your eyes. In the morning, it'll all be so different. I promise.

It's morning. Eleanor's awake, and propped up on one arm. It is a good arm. It is the best arm. She turns to Sam, who is absolutely not awake, in their bedroom, with its light-blocking curtains, for Sam is a shit sleeper. "Sam," says Eleanor, "I think that it isn't that a nuke is going to be dropped on New York. I mean I know that's what the President is saying, I know that's what the news is saying, but I feel like because they're saying it, I think everyone would see it coming, I think it would be scarier, I think it would be in a van, I think the reputation of vans will never recover, and I think that's really sad." Sam makes a noise, Eleanor pokes him, and Sam, eyes closed, says, "I think there should probably be a fallout shelter in the building, right? It used to be a hospital?" Sam opens one eye. Eleanor says to Sam, "This is absolutely something to look into, Sam." Sam opens the other eye. He loves her very much, and he is so very tired. Soon, Sam is going to look into this! What will he find? I'll tell you when he finds it! Later, it'll be dinner time, which is Sam's time to shine. Later, Eleanor will lean into him on the couch, which is the most expensive thing they have ever bought, and the first thing they ever bought together, which is another story I'll tell you, later, I promise, and she'll sigh, a really happy sigh, and put her hand on the couch, and feel how soft it is, how well it holds them, and she'll lean into Sam, and sigh, and he'll kiss her, right on the head. Soon I'll tell you all about it. At some point, the President is going to make some absolutely wild announcements that will only end in doom, which is a sentence no one has ever said before in the history of America, and I would know, because I looked it up, and I would never ever make up a story just to prove a point. Every night there will be dinner. Not in America, because of income inequality, but here, in the apartment where Sam and Eleanor live together, because Sam loves to cook Eleanor dinner, and to sit down together at the table they bought together, and to eat this dinner, together, as, outside the window, the snow falls.

Up in Heaven are the angels and then the rest of us are just here.

Maybe there are some things I should tell you first, while we're just here. I should probably tell you, while we're just here, that I'm telling you this story about Sam and Eleanor, and, as I'm telling you this story, sometimes I just want to talk to you, directly, outside of the story, and also inside the story, and so sometimes I can't remember the order things in the story happened, and sometimes it's important to hear them out of order because that's what the story needs, and anyway I'm doing the best I can with it, and trying to stay as true as I can to the heart of it. I'm doing the best I can. And I am so incredibly sorry if it's not enough. I just don't know how else to do this. And anyway this is a great time for the camera, the narrative, whatever, to zoom out, and for me to tell you about Sam and Eleanor.

Close your eyes. Picture a lake, with a beach, surrounded on all sides by trees, and grass, and cabins. Try to smell the water, and the grass, and see if you can tell if the grills are lit, and see if you can smell the sunscreen, and the sweat on your upper lip, and the beat of your heart.

The sun is out, the grass is green, your hair looks great, and you smell amazing.

Welcome to summer camp.

Sam and Eleanor met at summer camp. This was years ago. The sun was out and the grass was green and out on the lake were the canoes and on the shores was a cookout and even the air smelled alive. Earlier there had been a mock trial, and later everyone would really learn something. Meanwhile, there are hot dogs. Sam and Eleanor stand close enough to be holding hands, and then they are. After that, the sky splits open. It's a good start! It's a premise, at least.

Everyone's always writing letters at summer camp.

They're writing them in their bunks they're writing them at their desks they're writing them on hikes on paper on the backs of their knees where the skin is so smooth the ink just slides right off as you hike up your shorts, out there, in the woods, where we keep what's left of the mysteries. The greatest thing about summer camp is that nothing is like anything else and everything is covered in sweat and nothing, *not one single thing*, outside of this moment is real or of any actual consequence.

There's a lake. There's activities. There's the woods, where we keep what's left of the mysteries, stacked one on top of the other. In the woods things get stacked, one on top of the other. I don't know why. I'm not the woods. It has something to do, I think, with trees, and with the ways they can menace, how stacking things like mysteries or wolves one on top of the other forever in between the trees that were there when you were born and will be there when you die, cold, alone, having done nothing anyone will remember in fifty years, these trees that will still be standing, assuming the camp hasn't been turned into a golf course that will cost between $5,000 in the northern and easternmost states and $107,800 in the southwestern ones to keep watered every single year while small groups of people stand on them for no more than four hours at a time. It happens all over. The average golf course is maybe 150 acres, which amounts to about ninety-four city blocks. And none of this matters at summer camp! This is the beauty of summer camp! If the counselors weren't busy having rich inner lives, maybe things would be different, but they're not different, and wondering what things would be like if they were different really doesn't do any good, now does it? That's why there's a cookout. And activities. That's why the trees keep inching closer together. This is maybe the only time one thing is like something else at summer camp, is whenever the trees start to move.

Sam and Eleanor's parents worked hard to be able to afford to send their kids to summer camp in the summer so that said kids would have something to do, yes, but also so that their kids'd be out of the house and they, their parents, could, maybe!, for a little bit!, enjoy the summer for themselves and themselves alone for the first time in years. They missed their kids and all but as a parent it gets exhausting to be a parent. It's endless labor, more or less. And, again, your kids aren't paying their share of the rent. So Sam and Eleanor're at summer camp, they've been flirting for years and writing letters during the school year, like you do, but they've kept it up, which, as you know, dear reader, that's notable. That's a thing you notice. And so their hands noticed the other's, and were held, as the sky split open.

It is absolutely a fact that watching your whole entire summer camp drown in a lake during a storm straight out of the Bible is a deeply upsetting thing.

Years pass over days, days pass over years, whenever it was, this is what happens after. They wake up in their beds, at home. Their parents are weeping. Their sheets are soaked. I can't tell you how long it'll take to not feel like the world is falling down. And then, one day, the world stops falling down. Sometimes it works like that.

Sometimes it doesn't.

And, again, the years pass! They pass over high school over college over graduate school over parties over sex over the first time and how tender a mistake it is (Eleanor) and sudden and awkward and ecstatic it is (Sam) they pass over so many graduations and heartbreaks, over hunger and warmth, the years pass over snowstorms and squalls, they pass they pass they pass they pass, until, one day!, after the sky split open, but before the snow started falling, let's say this is five years ago, Sam walked into a party in Brooklyn one summer and there was Eleanor. "Hey," he said, "remember when the sky split open?" And then a light came on, and the sky split open.

Eleanor would tell him, at some point, that the thing about
that night, back when the sky cracked, was that it was nice
to remember what it's like to not know if the world will still
be there in the morning. Sam had something he wanted to say
but he couldn't figure out how to say it, and so his heart set
itself on fire in his chest, and grew wings, and a crown. I'm
trying to tell you that this was always going to happen, that it
was always going to be beautiful, and beset on all sides by a
sudden and certain doom. That's what I'm trying to tell you,
here. That's pretty much the whole point. Meanwhile whole
years pass. We shed so many cells. We've said so many things
we'll never remember. But here you are. "Sam," said Eleanor
at night, very early on, like maybe six months after that party,
while they were laying on top of Eleanor's bed in her studio
apartment with the bathroom that was as big as the rest of
the apartment, it was an incredible bathroom, and she never
again has a bathroom this nice, and a part of her will never let
that go, and that's fine, "Sam,

tell me a story."

OK SO IT'S THE FUTURE. The world has ended. Everyone and everything that ever was is a ghost, and they're all hanging out, just drifting through the ether, tethered to a longing they can never ever articulate. And so this one ghost goes up to another ghost and it tells the ghost a story. It's the only story in the whole world, and it is the saddest most beautiful story anyone has ever heard, it is just choking with beauty, this story, it is incredibly moving, and if you could have heard it, you would really finally truly and totally believe in love. OK so it's 1397. We're in Venice. Everything is made of marble, and the canals glisten under the moon, which watches us all. I wish you could see it. It'd just break your heart, how beautiful it all is. Across the street is Giovanni Medici. Hi, Giovanni! In a minute he's gonna start a bank and then, a little later, he's gonna buy the whole entire government, and a pope!, just to make sure that things just keep working out for him, and they absolutely keep working out for him and he really enjoys it and then he dies. OK so now it's the year 33. Jesus Christ has just convinced a really loud portion of the population of a pretty major city to love with an open heart and burn down the banks. The cops are furious about this because all cops hate love, so they get his friend to snitch on him so they can strap this fuckin guy to a pole and stab him to death. Later, after he's tied to a pole and stabbed to death till he dies and is buried in a cave or something, people claim to see Jesus around town, which freaks the cops out. They put everyone in prison and never let them out again. Anyway this is why his portrait hangs in every single bank, in hopes of warding off love, and revolt. Honestly, it's worked pretty well so far. OK so it's 1095. This one pope decides to retake the holy land and then everyone spends two hundred years in an on-again off-again relationship with burning the Middle East to the ground in a sort of If We Can't Have It Fuck You sort of way. All of a sudden, a boat of Christian soldiers marching on to war get very sick, on a boat, and die from their mouths, and nobody ever hears from them again. And so, since nobody ever hears from them again, the boat of Christian soldiers marching on to war on a boat can't warn anyone about scurvy, which is why, over the next three hundred years, like twenty million sailors die of scurvy, which is this disease that happens when you don't eat fresh vegetables, and what happens to you is first your gums go black and rot and bleed, and then you start bleeding from your scalp and you go through what doctors refer to as "emotional changes," while every wound you ever had on your body opens on up and begins to bleed more freely than you've ever done anything in your whole life, and it's called *scurvy*.

It's a really fun thing sometimes to think of a story as a unit of measure or distance.

And anyway, today, Sam went down to the basement, navigating the bizarre and endless Soviet-Bloc-style tunnels, still unsure where the fallout shelter was, until those tunnels spat him out into an unusable parking lot, to the right of which was the grocery store, where he bought a sack of mandarin oranges, which he put in a large bowl once he got home. At the grocery store, the newspapers were really worked up about the nuclear missile the President reminded everyone was headed towards New York City, but nobody had any explanation on why it hadn't gotten here yet, and when you asked about it, well, it was a bad idea to ask about it, and then Eleanor walked in the door to their apartment, where Sam currently was, and, seeing the mandarin oranges arrayed in the bowl, said, "Oh my God," and, "I love you," and, "How are we going to eat all of these, they'll go bad, they'll rot, they'll die, Sam," she says. "If we don't eat all these mandarin oranges you so thoughtfully bought, for nothing is as nice as the smell of citrus while the snow falls, if we don't eat them all before they rot, then someone you love will get scurvy, and they will die, and it will be terrible, for first their gums will turn black, and then bleed, and then their scalp will bleed, and they will go through what doctors refer to as 'emotional changes' and then every wound they have ever had will open up, and bleed, all that blood running from their body like their body was a house on fire, Sam, and they will die, and it will be terrible," and Sam says, "Oh no," for he knows that this is true, and that Eleanor does not make the rules, and there is no use arguing. In the morning, the sun breaks its way into the kitchen in a real spiritual sort of way. In the corner, a rubber tree plant is shedding itself of all its worldly possessions. In the morning, at the table, Sam and Eleanor sit holding hot mugs of coffee to their faces. Between them is the bowl of mandarins. They stay like that all day. The sun doesn't move. The rubber tree plant is completely devoid of all possessions. It grows new leaves. The old ones burst into flames and head on up to Heaven, with the angels, who are singing, soft and low, like a hymn. Eleanor walks out the door and goes to work. Sam just sits there. Eleanor comes right back. It's Sunday. People died so Eleanor wouldn't have to work today. She sits down. "People died so I wouldn't have to work today," she says. She's still sitting down. She's shocked. She just came home from work on Friday, and the day had been so long, and the mandarin oranges were there, and everything was beautiful, and smelled like winter, and now all of a sudden and with no warning it's Sunday. Do you understand the passing of time? Me neither! Meanwhile, Sam refills her coffee and eases her coat off her back and onto the rack they hung over one of the doors for when guests come over, so they can put their coats somewhere. "Thanks," says Eleanor. She means it so much. He took her coat away and gave her more coffee. She doesn't have to do anything today. She can just sit here until the moon comes out. Sam'll make lunch, and then Sam'll make dinner. She'll look at her phone to see if there's anything new about the nuclear missile. It's closer to possible, today. She looks up payloads and closes the tab. Outside the snow will fall. They'll play Scrabble and she'll beat the shit out of him. They'll stand up. They'll go to the bathroom and brush their teeth, they'll wash their faces, they'll do a clay mask, it'll get hot, they'll wash it off, they'll apply toner then lotion, they'll admire their pores, they'll take off all their clothes, and they'll get into bed. This was their whole day, and now it's over. Outside it's snowing. Years ago there was a party in a house that was covered in these small trees. You could barely find the door. The basement was fully carpeted with a bar in the corner. The lighting upstairs was soft, and everyone's hair was enormous and perfect. They were all talking about the future. This made everyone feel alive until they didn't, and after that they went to work, and then the world ended. Up in Heaven, the natives, who are angels, were getting restless. They kept lighting their swords on fire and packing into the bedroom of one of Heaven's smallest apartments. Meanwhile, Sam and Eleanor are asleep. The snow is falling. In the middle of the night Eleanor wakes up. She had the strangest dream. "Sam," she says, softly. "Sam." And Sam, who is basically asleep, tells her that the city always leaves the streetlights on at night. In case the angels come.

I wouldn't say that Sam believes in angels, but I would say that Sam believes that, when the world ends, the angels will, finally, come. What does that mean? I really don't know at the moment, but I'm genuinely excited to find out.

Sam put some chicken thighs in a Dutch oven on a low heat which he salted and peppered while he diced up some garlic. Once the chicken smelled like it'd started to brown he moved it around and made a hole for the garlic to go, and once the garlic smelled like it'd started to brown he took some tongs and turned the chicken around and salted and peppered it again. He added a two-to-one mix of cider vinegar and soy sauce. He added three or four bay leaves and a baker's dozen peppercorns. He poured some tonic water into some Madeira and he stared at the wall. In the other room his phone made a noise, and he started in on the rice. Somewhere there were some sugar snaps, waiting to be steamed, ever so lightly, with a splash, just a splash!, of sesame oil. Eleanor walked through the door. Dinner was on the table.

After dinner, Sam and Eleanor put on that movie they like, the one that's incredibly sweet, you know the one, it's a love story for the ages, there is no threat of nuclear disaster aside from the ever-present one of living in a time when people can launch nuclear weapons at each other whenever and just annihilate life, there's a bank robbery, there are a lot of bank robberies, which result in the end of debt in America, then they shoot a thousand cops, and then the sky cracks open, and it's over, that's it, that's the end, just like in all the best stories. It's a really exciting and heart-warming movie. I can't believe you haven't seen it. Meanwhile, Eleanor turns to Sam, and unbuttons his shirt, which she is wearing. Beneath it is a sheer black bra. The lights go dim. The camera pans away. In the grocery store there is a sale on milk. At the end of the sale, all unbought milk will be taken out back, and shot. It's rough out there in the free market, folks! In the end, it comes for us all. Back in the grocery store, families wander, lit terribly from above as children run through the aisles, grabbing at the shelves, they're growing right before our eyes, they **need new** pants, their voices are dropping, it is really exciting, **their parents** are thrilled! Down the street the union organizers gather in the bar. They chant solidarity, forever. The landlords are all around. There is blood on their teeth. They are heavily involved in some plots. If you were to ask me what I mean by that I would tell you that once there was this one writer who said that a plot was a parcel of land which you are eventually put down into. Either way, I love you with all my heart.

Way out in America, while Sam was desperately eating a mandarin to stave off the death of a loved one, Eleanor was dreaming about a vacation. It was so beautiful. The sun was everywhere. When she woke, the world nearly broke her heart.

The streetlights are on. It is 3:30 in the afternoon. I meant to turn them off when I went to work in the morning, but now it's dark, so.

You're welcome.

"Today," says the President, "the threat of a nuclear strike on New York City by foreign powers is at the highest it has ever been in national history." It is absolutely worth noting that 42 percent of the nuclear arsenal *in the entire world* is held by the United States. (The US has 5,550; Russia has 6,255; France has 290; China has 350; The UK has 225; Pakistan has 165; India has 156; Israel has 90; and North Korea has 40. Nine countries possess the entirety of the world's nuclear arsenal, and two of them make up 91 percent. Why? Honestly, why?) There have been maybe ten close calls with nuclear strikes in America, two of which occurred during the Cuban Missile Crisis, and once, on the 15th of April in 1969, when the President ordered a nuclear strike against North Korea, as a joke, when he was drunk.

OK so the thing about the President, and I guess it's time I tell you about this, because the thing about the President is that the President has always been the President, and will always be the President, and after the President dies there'll be another President, forever, until the end of the world, upon whose dread glory the critics remain, to this day, divided. I mean that once you're elected President you're only ever referred to as the President. Yes it's confusing, but so is democracy, so I really don't see what you're complaining about.

Meanwhile, the President gets a haircut. It's dawn. He calls his wife, who dies. It is pretty much a tragedy. Then he has lunch. Lunch involves prawns. His mouth is absolutely, positively, full. Then there are meetings. The meetings suck. The gist of the meetings is that, right now, everything sucks. Oh well! Sometimes that happens! Now it's night. In his bed, the President sleeps, alone, with the news. In the middle of the night the President is assassinated. In the morning, nothing changes. In the morning, the President wakes up in the body of an oil tycoon, but the oil tycoon dies. In the morning, the President wakes up in the body of an international assassin who assassinates a President who is not this President, but is *a* President, and soon after that the international assassin is assassinated in a hotel by drowning in his bathtub alone. In the morning, the President wakes up in the body of a high school quarterback seconds before a traumatic brain injury. Then the President wakes up in the body of a surface-to-air missile and just sits there for fifteen years until he explodes, taking with him a school, and killing hundreds of children in an air strike. The President weeps alone in a room for waiting while angels pretend not to notice. They contain a malicious sort of grace. Meanwhile, the President wakes up in the body of a tuba player the President wakes up in the body of the news the President wakes up in the body of debt itself, which will consume us all, and he lives like that forever until the world ends and then, after the world ends, the President wakes up in the body of the beach at sunset on the most romantic night of your life. Everything goes dark. The President wakes up in the body of the President but he has to go. The President is ripped away from us all.

It's too hot in the bedroom, because in New York the landlord holds the thermostat, so Sam gets up and opens a window. "Open it wider," says Eleanor, who Sam thought was asleep. He checks the humidifier, which is empty. It is not enough. The window isn't open enough, the humidifier isn't humid enough, the cold isn't cold enough, nothing could ever possibly be enough. His sinuses are a vast and arid desert, as barren as the fucking plains. He goes online and buys a new humidifier, one with an incredible coverage capacity. Their ceilings are too high. When the new humidifier, sleek, white, tall, with a wide and easy-to-clean mouth finally comes, as was promised and foretold by the internet, they can use the old one for guests, or for the plants, or the office. They moved into this apartment for the office. Eleanor asks Sam what he's doing. Technically the office is a bedroom, for the purposes of billing, and, technically, it could be, if you were, like, a small child and therefore unable to contribute to the rent. Technically, Eleanor is asleep. The old humidifier can go in there, in the office. Sam refills the old humidifier and drops in some bacteriostatic fluid because he heard he is supposed to. Back in the bedroom he holds his phone up to the humidifier and checks the filter. Eleanor rolls over in her sleep in bed. Sam could be in bed. It looks nice and promises naught but tenderness. In the morning Sam will have to close the window, because it will be freezing. Sam gets in bed. He holds on to Eleanor for dear life. It is absolutely incredible. Up in their homes are the landlords. Who even knows what they're doing there. It is four in the morning. Nobody is being arrested right now, so there's that. Interest rates are holding. Jobs exist, and, if you want, we can prove it. Plus, nobody in this room has thought about a nuclear bomb going off all day, the 3 train is delayed, indefinitely, the G train is in the river, we don't know which one, if we did, it wouldn't be in the river still, now would it? Up in the sky is the moon. Is the moon a snitch? It's hard to say. The moon conducts the tides, which pull at our hearts, day and night. A whole bunch of babies are, this instant!, born, screaming, each and every one of them. Good luck out there, babies! I hope your parents love you very much, and that the cops don't shoot you! I hope you're never scared of money, and that you never have to decide between rent or groceries! I hope the moon speaks to you, and that, when it does, you listen. The moon is not a snitch. I'm sorry I said that earlier. I take it back. Go to sleep. Close your eyes. In the morning, the world will still be here. I'm sorry. I promise.

It's evening. There's a bar. Eleanor and Sam are there, talking about those movies, the ones where the world ends, with all those people who just go on, who brave the wasteland to carry the spark of humanity for the future, which is sure to come, which they will build with their blood and gild with their shining white bones. It is insane to behave like that. Think about the dinosaurs! They knew what to do when the world ends. Boy fucking howdy. All around them are people, sitting, standing, drinking, someone is getting empanadas, then everyone is getting empanadas. The snow is falling all around. Do you know what I'm talking about? It's the end of the world. Not now, I mean, picture this: It's the end of the world. How much of your life are you happy with?

Now it's tomorrow, and the world's still here. Some of the ways it has ended before are as follows: floods, meteor strike, asteroid strike, total climate collapse, the first trees bleeding acid into the bedrock to turn it into soil flooding the atmosphere with things the atmosphere did not yet have a name for while in the depths of the sea all life was boiled alive, there was this one film series where it's never really clear what happened but with the way people feel about rape and gasoline and violence it also maybe seems like maybe the explanation is already there, when the asteroid that killed the dinosaurs hit it was so big and so fast that the atmosphere ripped open and the crater formed before it even hit and it is highly likely that dinosaurs were ripped through the vacuum of space and hurtled onto the moon along with whatever else but what really spelled the end of the world was that all of India was a super-volcano and it went off at the same time as the asteroid hit and scientists say that what happened when it hit was that if you could see it you were already dead.

Anyway Eleanor was reading a book on all the ways the world has ended, and also the end of the world was, in general, on the minds of every New Yorker, due to the President reminding us, every day, that, now, more than ever, we could be hit by a nuclear missile, launched by a foreign power, and headed right for us.

Sam didn't have enough money to be able to make lamb shanks braised in tomatoes and garlic and onions and rosemary and thyme and a dry white wine for dinner tonight and it was a fucking tragedy. He looked at his phone, whose lock screen was a picture of Eleanor, as a toddler, with a hastily applied red lip, and screaming. He could weep, he loved her so much. So he did. Sam stood in the grocery store, and he wept. Soon everyone in the grocery store was weeping. The world is just too much sometimes! And that is OK! This was the weeping report, sorry it was so short. Meanwhile, Sam still had to figure out what to make for dinner. What are you doing to make for dinner, Sam? Sam, in response, wept.

Meanwhile Eleanor was at work.

The snow fell all around. Every morning in winter the world was really something. Beneath Eleanor's office was a day care or a child store. All the children were lined up in the window, playing or screaming or eating or napping. They were building whole worlds and holding local elections. If you looked in their eyes long enough you could see their hopes and their dreams spilling out their mouths like ghosts in cartoons as your heart changed size to hold all the feelings you had for them, and you could see them seeing this, and you'd know the day, to the minute, when they'd bury you. The world was full of so many things!

Eleanor walked over to the window and stood there as children dove out of windows. Eleanor held her breath. They landed in a snowfall two stories down. They screamed the whole way down and they didn't even die and they lay there laughing. They made a promise with the world and the world kept it and if that wasn't a miracle then miracles don't exist and you can just go home and die. Did they know about the nuke? What kind of parent would terrorize a kid with that? While she was thinking about this, the ceiling tore open, and the angels came, like we'd always been promised they would.

Meanwhile, Sam was roasting a chicken.

He'd brined it for two hours in sugar and salt and patted it dry and slipped hunks of butter under the skin and sprinkled it with salt and pepper, and the chicken was sitting on a beer can so the beer in the can could baste the chicken and Sam had put the skins of the mandarins in the beer can as he ate the last of them, comforted by the fact that no one he loved would die, horribly, of scurvy, because of him, and beneath the chicken, in the broiler pan, were potatoes Sam'd pre-boiled a bit that were cooking in the fat that was falling. Everything smelled delicious. Sam was cutting broccoli off the stalks and tossing them in a pan with oil and salt and some red pepper flakes. Eleanor walked through the door and said, "Hi, baby. I know I'm home early, and that this is an unexpected delight for you," and it was. She said, "You see, I was borne home on the backs of angels. They tore open the building, and deposited me here." Sam thought about this. He looked up from the broccoli and said, "So do you have to go in tomorrow?" "No, Sam. There is no more work, and there is no more tomorrow, for we are all of us, now and forever, children in the kingdom of Heaven on Earth." Sam thanked God for burning down the banks just like His only Son had tried to do over two thousand years ago. It was at this point that Eleanor said she was joking and Sam said he knew that, but honestly I'm not so sure he did. If the world was ending, then the angels would come. Right?

Eleanor left work early today because she was worried about the trains, which were, at 3:30 in the afternoon, already running with thirty-minute delays. It took her two hours to make a thirty-five-minute commute. Eleanor hoped this was not indicative of things to come, although she did in fact know better, but when she came home dinner was ready, so it all worked out in the end, and nobody died of scurvy that night.

The other night Eleanor came so hard the world shifted.

That was the only way they could think to describe it.

This was the winter they started trying to do Shabbat. Sam knew the first verse. Eventually he'll get the rest. It's a nice thing to do, as the sun sets, to welcome the weekend, is to light a candle and say a prayer. In theory this represents the pinnacle of the creation of the universe. It's a nice thought, to watch the candles burn, while the snow falls. Eleanor felt closer to a life she barely knew. Sam felt closer to Eleanor. The snow felt closer to everyone that winter. It just never stopped.

I should also mention that lighting a candle together as the sun sets on a Friday in winter while commuting from Manhattan to Brooklyn is absolutely a little ambitious.

OK so it's 1587. The beach in Virginia is shit. The sun's too cold, the sand's a swamp, the fish are mosquitoes, your bed's a grave. It's a bad time, all around, to be honest. This is why Roanoke packed its ass up and moved to Jersey, without leaving so much as a forwarding address, because they didn't know how to write, because they were fucking morons. They found this long sliver of land off the shore. It had a beach and a bay. There were some people there, but they're gone now. And when death comes, death comes wearing such a fine white hat, with such beautiful flowers, spelling your name. OK so it's 1851. I walk over to a cow and I cut two real choice cuts of meat from it. I build a fire and grill them, seasoned with salt and pepper and thyme. We have mashed potatoes and those skinny green beans cooked lightly in browned butter and a bit of lemon. I set this meal out for us on a table with a gingham cloth overlooking the Pacific Ocean, which could split you in two if you'd just ask. One day all of this will be under water.

Sam turns on the news. IN CENTRAL PARK, THE SNOW HAS REACHED TWO TO THREE FEET. A MOUNTAIN RANGE HAS FORMED. ONE COLLAPSED ONTO A TODDLER AND THEN THE TODDLER'S LUNGS COLLAPSED. EXPERTS BELIEVE THESE EVENTS TO BE RELATED. "Jesus," says Sam. I'LL SAY, says the news. The news is dressed up as a stern man in a suit. THE FORECAST IS GRIM, says the news. "I get it," says Sam. The news is dressed up as a blonde. The news is a radio. The news says, THE MOUNTAIN RANGES HAVE BEGUN TO BE NAMED. THEIR HEIGHTS ARE CURRENTLY INCALCULABLE. IF ONLY YOU COULD JUST SETTLE DOWN, SAM, AND LIVE A LIFE FREE OF DEBT OR WORRY, THINGS MIGHT RETURN TO NORMAL,

TO SOME SEMBLANCE OF REASONABILITY THAT WE COULD
ALL SURVIVE. The news looks Sam dead in the eye. THAT WE
COULD ALL. SURVIVE. Sam looks away.

"Sam," says Eleanor, "Did you ever figure out about a fallout shelter?" He did. "I did, baby." "OK, please tell me all
about it!" "Well there's a fallout shelter in the basement,"
Sam had followed the signs for it. "I followed the signs for
the shelter," and then he found it, "and then I found it," but
here's the thing, is that the fallout shelter, maybe six years
ago, was turned into an apartment, "and they just told me
their rent is going up, which is weird, since their lease isn't
up, and this is rent stabilized, so we're all going to go to the
tenant's union about this, but, in the meantime, I'm sorry,
but, I think if the bomb goes off we'll just die." "Well, I
mean, at least we'll be together." "We will absolutely be together!" "And then we'll be dead." They will absolutely be
dead if a nuclear blast goes off, and if it does, they had better run towards it, because death from exposure is horrific,
it is absolutely one of the worst ways to go, it is so fucking
awful I absolutely do not even want to try to describe it, I
don't want to picture it, just pray that it's fast. Please, God,
let it be fast.

I'm not saying that angels haven't interfered in the course of
human history I'm just saying that if the world was going to
end then that's what's going to happen, and in the meantime
we should do everything we can to stop the world from end-

ing, to love each other as best we can, and to try to give value and meaning to each and every life, except for cops, whose lives have no meaning. That's all I'm trying to say.

Anyway, Sam and Eleanor are having a really stupid conversation. Eleanor's worried about the impending nuclear strike on New York City that the President makes a point of mentioning every day, and Sam didn't seem to be really worried about it, and Eleanor said, and I can't tell you if she meant it, I think she was just trying to get the conversation to go somewhere, that sometimes it felt like Sam wasn't ever thinking about the impending nuclear strike that could wipe out the city of New York, where they lived!, and Sam wanted to prove he did think about these things, and so he talked about a movie, and Three Mile Island, and how that went was Eleanor gave him a kiss to shut him up. It's hard to imagine dying. It makes you think about all this shit you don't want to think about. Remember that episode where the local billionaire nuclear power plant owner is found floating in the woods, glowing green with radiation, and, mistaken for an angel, tells the townsfolk, *I bring you love*, and the townsfolk say, *It brings us love! Kill it!*

I think about that a lot.

I might be remembering that wrong but, outside of a court of law, I think you'll have a hard time proving it.

Eleanor's sitting at the window, whose sill is two feet deep, watching the snow fall. Sam's sitting in bed, watching her watching the snow. Earlier she was easing him into her. She held his shoulders down and told him not to move a fucking inch, and he didn't. But now it's now, and the snow is, still, falling. Eleanor's still sitting on the sill in the morning while the sun rises. She couldn't sleep, and she watched the snow fall, all night long, and the whole entire city was completely beautiful for almost exactly two hours. Sam brought her coffee, or he stayed in bed. I can't tell you everything that happens. I'm sorry.

Up in Heaven were the angels. They were tired. There was a choir. All was grace and light and awe. Everything was clean and smelled amazing, in that it smelled like nothing. The angels were tired of being invoked left and right. It was exhausting. So they turned off all the lights in Heaven. Every angel went into the bedroom. They were all packed in there. Fiery swords and all. The light of Heaven is within you. You sad sad fuck.

Once upon a time before they moved their lives into the same series of rooms, Sam came over to Eleanor's apartment and she was in the bath. Her building had a doorman and she told Sam to just walk in like he owned the place. So he dressed up his face like he'd never known an overdraft fee and just walked on in there. Everyone waved at him and smiled. Sam got in the elevator. He walked to her door. He opened the door. She was in the bath and he called out, "Hey?" and in response she said the sound of water filling a tub. The whole apartment filled with water. Then the sky split open.

Can you see where I'm going with this?

I **DON'T KNOW** why all of the angels in Heaven were all packed up in the bedroom of the smallest one-bedroom apartment in the kingdom of Heaven. I don't know why they stayed there like that, with their flaming swords of judgment on fire like that so that then of course their wings were also on fire like that, which led to the smoke alarm going off over and over like that, when just outside their room there was an endless banquet and a hundred gilded bathrooms. So, yes, when the angels do, finally, come, they'll probably be fucking jerks about it, molting all of your hardwood floors, setting off your fire alarms, bringing down the property values, and absolutely waking the baby. Meanwhile, downstairs on Earth, Sam says to Eleanor, "Hey, has anyone ever told you," and Eleanor says, "Sam, do not even think about it."

Eleanor went over to Sam, who was sitting on the couch, staring at the snow fall, with a look on his face, and she sat on his lap, facing him, and kissed him, long, and deep. The snow kept falling. Student loans continued to accrue interest at life-shattering rates. In the fall, before the snow fell, the whole city had risen, as one, and marched in the streets against police violence, as the police drove their cars into the crowd, killing even more people. Nobody stopped marching. Eleanor was not about to stop kissing Sam. Sam was not about to stop kissing Eleanor. The police are not about to stop killing you. There is literally no one stopping them. "What's for dinner?" asked Eleanor. "That," said Sam, catching his breath, "is an incredible question."

Later they'd watch that movie where, for a moment, the two outlaws build a home in the trees and dance the day away. There's something really beautiful about a love story where two cute teens who know nothing of the world but their love drive around and kill cops. It's not a story that can ever really go anywhere because if it went somewhere then we'd have to look at them as something other than aberrations to be corrected. But it's a really beautiful movie. And if you've ever been in love as a teenager and watched as the whole world was swept away by a flood that fell from the sky and together you built a house in the trees for weeks till someone came to rescue you, then part of this movie might really speak to you on a level you are incapable of articulating. And for everyone else, it's still beautiful. All of these lands are bad, and nobody ever gets out alive in America.

That was earlier, now we're here. Now the sun's up. Now Johnny's been at work for an hour. Now Jane's awake. You'll meet them later. Now the news says the Attorney General will shoot someone on live TV. Now the news is just kidding. Now it's not. Now you've had breakfast. Now your heart aches, for reasons you couldn't give voice to if you tried! The world is just so much right now, and it always will be! Forever! How about that???? But wait! Now a train's hurtling through darkness and out onto a bridge! Sam's phone shouts I LOVE YOU in his pocket! Sam descends once more into darkness, and then, later, into the light! We all contain the miraculous inside of us! It is really something!

Sam is, at the moment, almost entirely out of work. He is freelancing as a proofreader and fact-checker for places on the internet. Sometimes he has enough money to take Eleanor out for dinner, and sometimes she has to get the groceries this month. It isn't the best feeling, not knowing what you'll have beyond rent each month. The President cut unemployment down to a month. The President felt that anyone who couldn't get a job in a month just wasn't trying hard enough. Meanwhile the trains are fucked, the pipes are frozen, the heat is too strong, the cops are shooting children in the street, all the vegetables look sad, it is not exactly Christmas, but tonight Sam and Eleanor are going to get dinner with Johnny and Jane, and won't that be nice?

It is an absolutely terrible feeling to realize that you are barely able to support yourself and that there seems to be absolutely nothing you can do about it. I just wanted you to understand that.

Jane and Johnny are their friends who are also a couple. They have other friends who are couples, but Jane and Johnny are the ones who, when they first started dating, they felt closest to! Jane and Johnny have been together, off and on, since high school. They're the only people outside their parents who know how Sam and Eleanor met. It just isn't a story they love to tell. It's traumatic, it's difficult to believe, and it casts their love as this fated thing, rather than what it is, which is two people trying to build a life together, side by side, here in America, before the world ends. Jane is a lawyer and Johnny works in fine art installation. Johnny went to art school, and so did Sam, and they only really talk about it together at this point, how early their foundation courses were, why people even go to art school (I could not tell you, only to say that there are many ways you can learn to devote your life in service to the notion of art's capacity for transcendence), why art schools always had very competitive kickball teams (it's easier to smoke while playing kickball), shit like that. Johnny did not make art anymore. Johnny really loved his job. Jane and Johnny loved spending time with Sam and Eleanor because they loved watching how much they loved each other and because they were easy to talk to. Sam loved spending time with them because he felt like it was a good example for how things could work based on how things were in their life. Eleanor loved spending time with them because she loved Jane, and she loved Johnny, and she loved Sam, and she hoped that Sam could see something in the ways they accepted each other's lives so that he would maybe both accept his own life, and also grow beyond it. I don't really know how else to explain it right now. I am sure they'll get into an argument about it and then it'll make more sense. That's what tends to happen with these sorts of things!

Sam had to go into the city for a meeting this morning. There were so many office buildings, the city was just lousy with office buildings today, of all days, and all of their windows kept reflecting the sun back and forth into Sam's eyes, forever. In the middle of the meeting the managing editor, without saying a word, rose to her feet. She walked over to her desk and set her computer on fire. Everyone sort of lost track of her after that. And anyway there was still about two hours' worth of meeting left. Sam, though a freelancer!, was important enough to have to come to the meeting and stand in the corner, shifting his weight from one foot to the other. Sam was blinking, and hungry, and several articles were planned regarding a nuclear strike on New York City, but it was starting to feel like nobody's heart was really in it anymore, and there was this great pitch about what if we just welcome death, and there wasn't lunch, and there wasn't water, and there wasn't any coffee, and then it was over, and when he got home, Sam would learn that he was not going to be paid for attending the meeting, and also there would not be any work for him this month, but they were so very grateful that he was such a team player and made the trip up! Meanwhile the police shot someone outside, the copy chief was weeping, and so were the sprinklers. Because of the computer that was set on fire. Things had, on the whole, once, been better than they were right now. Pretty much everyone could agree on this.

While Sam was in his meeting Eleanor sat at her desk in her open-plan office while her boss sat at her desk in her private office, thinking up the most beautiful, nested paywalls the internet had ever seen. Their subtlety would be magnificent, Eleanor's boss thought. It was entirely possible no one would ever even figure out the way the paywall worked. The whole world could change. People could only see what they could afford to see. Eleanor's boss could barely contain herself. She strode out of the office with a great and magnificent purpose.

Eleanor watched her go. Johnny was inside a vast and endless chasm. At the other end was a sound that would change someone's life. It could be said that museums were a sort of refuge, but I am not going to be the person saying that when you think about what it was that they bought all that art with. Jane was in a team meeting that wasn't a team meeting so much as it was a private meeting, and it wasn't a private meeting so much as it was an empty conference room with the lights off, and the room utterly empty, aside from the partner who called the meeting, who was beckoning for Jane to sit down, and there was only one chair, and he was in it. Jane was trying to do the math on where they could have put all the chairs so quickly and with such efficiency. She realized there were probably hidden closets in the room. This unnerved her. Outside was the city. It was absolutely full of people.

Off in the distance, the landlords laughed and laughed and laughed and laughed!

Sam left the city at two. THE TRAINS, THEY ARE SO FUCKED, JUST LIKE YOU WILL BE WHEN THE BOMBS FALL, AND THEY WILL, ANY DAY NOW, said the radio, YOU CANNOT BELIEVE HOW LUCKY YOU WERE THAT IT ONLY TOOK YOU TWO HOURS TO GET HOME. SOON, said the radio, NOT NOW, BUT SOON, IT WILL TAKE DAYS FOR TRAINS TO CROSS THE RIVERS. YOU'D BE BETTER OFF ON HORSEBACK, said the radio, YOU'D BE BETTER OFF AS A BIRD. YOUR WHOLE LIFE COULD BE SO DIFFERENT, YOU COWARDS.

Fuck the police. Really and truly, fuck them. Fucking cowards.

Eleanor texted Sam to say that she was on the train, but it was not moving. Meanwhile, the apartment was so very hot. Sam opened a window. He sat down at the table. He leaned back. He closed his eyes. The sun was setting! *Shit!* thought Sam! He got the candles ready. He got out his phone. *Baruch atah Adonai Eloheinu melech ha-olam asher kid'shanu b'mitzvotav v'tzivanu l'hadlik neir shel Shabbat.* Eleanor was still on the train where she was still reading that book about all the ways the world has ended and will end again someday. Once upon a time the trees had to bleed acid into the bedrock to turn it into soil, into something like a home. It's weird to think about burning down the land to live in it until you think about America. Johnny picked up Jane from work on his motorcycle.

Meanwhile, in Yemen, due to US-backed Saudi blockades, nearly 400,000 children die of starvation. Saudi Arabia, back in 2015, wanted to interfere in the Yemeni civil war to produce an outcome favorable to them, and they do have all the oil we need, and so, and this is absolutely a massive simplification on my part, the blockade that all the Presidents support, have supported, and will support, as the President is indeed a perpetual object in perpetual motion, leads to nearly 400,000 children dying of starvation. Anyway, tonight, in Brooklyn, as people made it home, the windows all around the block lit up, in minor ways, the too-sudden dusk.

Meanwhile Sam was standing outside the Italian place that
used to be a Senegalese place a few blocks over. He and Eleanor were meeting Jane and Johnny for dinner soon. It was eight.
The snow was still falling. The wind screamed for a bit and
things got terrifying. Mountains of snow taller than cars, taller
than people, were falling, and then the car alarms were screaming, and people were screaming for the cars to stop screaming,
but nobody could hear them over the cars, or the wind. Sam
wished Eleanor was here, and then she was. Earlier today Eleanor had pricked her finger and written Sam's name on her desk,
where she earned all their money. When she finally got off the
train at Franklin and waited for the shuttle to take her back up
near Prospect, she got the text, and watched Sam lighting the
candles, and saying the prayer, for her, for their home, for their
future, for the weekend, which was sure to come.

Dinner was delicious. They split two amazing salads of little
gems and marcona almonds and some goat cheese and honey
and quick-pickled red onions, some meatballs with some weird
pesto made from I want to say like maybe broccolini?, and
some incredible arancini. Then Sam had an oxtail ravioli in
a marrow sauce with a little fried sage, Eleanor had linguine
with burnt vanilla beans and lobster, Johnny had this duck
ragu with these thick ridged noodles that were definitely not
spaghetti but I don't know how else to describe them but they
were not unlike a very thick very ridged and absolutely perfect
spaghetti noodle, and Jane had the single greatest vegetarian
lasagna of her life. They had this wild orange wine Jane kept
getting more bottles of while Sam stared at a point in the

distance. Eleanor put her hand over his, and he turned to face her, and she was smiling. Everyone had been talking about their days but I already told you about them and I didn't think you needed to sit through it all again. Then Sam and Eleanor started talking about this movie they'd seen, the one where it's all sunsets and horses, where love is the sort of thing you could choke on. At one part, the happy couple is riding along, and then there's just this sea of horses. They're everywhere. The camera keeps pulling back and back and back, and it's just horses, flooding the screen, forever. The sound is deadening. You know the lovers are saying something sacred to each other. You can almost hear it. After that everyone sort of sat there for a minute. Last night Johnny watched a documentary called *One Day All Your Cities Will Be Salt*. It was about how one day all our cities will be salt. The angels will never come. Nothing we've ever done will last, not even our bones. The dead we've piled like so many trophies to record our glory meant nothing. Salt. That's it. Johnny said he thought in a week or so everyone would stop talking about the nuke, and we'd all just forget we thought it was gonna happen in the first place. Jane got up and quietly paid the check after going to the bathroom. Then, the lights went out, and so did everyone else. The staff stayed and cleaned everything. They all shared a cigarette out back, one after the other. They waded in the water, together, having cleaned the mats, and then God troubled the water, and then, after that, it's anyone's guess.

On the way home Eleanor put her head on Sam's shoulder, and leaned in close like he could save her whole life, and Sam leaned in and kissed her on her head, which was covered in a hat under a hood under the pile of snow that had gathered during the three-block walk, and then, dear reader, they were home, and out of their coats, at which point it turned out that Sam had to dig them a path through the living room to the bedroom, because, it turned out, the living room was full of snow!, because, it turned out, earlier it was hot and someone, it is a real mystery who it could have been, had opened a window, and the snow did fall and fall and fall through the window into the living room and now here we are, trying to get to bed. (It's really amazing how the couch wasn't ruined by all the snow. It was not a cheap couch. They had really spent some money on it. They saved up for months and months. They went to the couch store and said, "We would like to buy a beautiful couch, please!" and the couch store just laughed and laughed at them, and it was awful, and they went home and sat down in Sam's two low-slung yellow chairs, and they wept. But now they have a perfect couch, so suck on that.) Inside the apartment, the snow was gone and the couch was a miracle. Outside, the wind was howling, and everything had turned to ice. In their warm dry bed Sam told Eleanor a story about the two of them except that all of his parts were played by the fallow fields in winter and all of her parts were played by the workers of the world, united. That's just how it was: bombs burst like a song, and all the dreams you ever had just walked into the sea, and the workers of the world, united, made love to the fallow fields in winter so tenderly that the world ended.

I don't know how else to put it.

I love you with all my heart.

SOMETIMES IT'S JUST SO HARD to sit down across from someone with all of their feelings all over their face and then you have to eat dinner like that with your feelings like that and you have a little drink like that with your feelings like that and then there you are, drunk, with your feelings, and with the check still to come and you think maybe *hey do I have enough for this in checking right now?*, and you look at your phone for answers, like as though anything in the world would have an answer. The dinner date was invented so long ago we don't even have a year for it. What happened was one person asked the person if they wanted to get dinner, and the other person said yes. Nobody tells this story because nobody dies and there aren't any explosions. I think there has to be a better way to tell it, where we can all just appreciate things a little more. There has to be.

Right?

Both Johnny and Jane went home alone because nobody knew they'd broken up. One day they just woke up and felt like strangers living inside a life they'd built together, and it was scary. It was scary to look into the eyes of the person whose health insurance you were on every morning and have her look at you like a stranger. It was fucking scary to come home every day to the man who built your table your bed your couch your life, who'd scaffolded up your sense of self for five years, and have him tell you when you come home from the job that pays for his motorcycle insurance and gas, that he hadn't even the inkling of a notion of how to start to talk to you now. So Jane called a car and Johnny, whose motorcycle was now out of gas, and who decided to simply leave it at the restaurant, like the first bit of his life he was getting ready to walk away from, rode a bus to a train and read an article on his phone about the tidal wave that would, one day, destroy the entire west coast. The tidal wave, Johnny read, wouldn't look like a painting; it'd be a sea of cars and buildings rising up and folding in on itself, forever. Johnny texted Jane, because who else could he tell this to? Who else in the whole world could he just talk to about all the things in his head and what was he going to do now?, *A sea of cars and buildings rising up and folding in on itself, forever*, and she texted him back, *An infinite void in the shape of the idea of California*, and he smiled, and looked out the bus. Outside the bus was an army on horseback, all bugles and bayonets, their coats all rotten with blood, all sagging in the snow and the dirty rain falling from the clouds that hung over all our heads that fateful night, and then they hooked a right on Union down towards the river, Jane texted, *Just saw a cannon being pulled down Flatbush, drifting west*, and Johnny texted her back a flood of horses and Jane was typing, for a while, Johnny's heart got a little rush, but nothing happened, in the middle of the night, he'd text her, *I can't keep doing this. I just can't.*, but now, Jane's phone was a sea of horses, it was a flood of horses, until all her phone could see was horses, until all she could see was horses, until the cab was full of horses, and her whole world was a sea of stampeding horses, stampeding her off to her apartment, to bed, and then there they were, a room full of horses, and it's two it's three it's four it's five it's six in the morning, and nobody has made coffee, and she's all alone, except for her whole entire apartment full of horses she's going to have to walk through if she ever wants to get anywhere again, the horses, who are running over the bridge and the snow and your dreams and the landlords, they are coming, the horses, for you, and downstairs outside some asshole teenagers are waiting for a bus and pelting this ball against the dying metal sign that says BUS over and over and over and over and over again and, I swear to God, it sounds like victory, like there's blood in the air, and the sun would just burn your eyes out if only you'd let it.

I've been trying so hard to tell you how much I love you. I've been trying to tell you using America. Maybe this is why it keeps coming out wrong. I'm sorry. I love you. I wish I knew why this keeps happening, and I'm going to try to do better next time. I hope tonight your dreams come easy, and wondrous, and prepare you completely for the world to come.

Sometimes it's easier to talk to a person when you don't have to look at them and see the history of your whole life in their eyes. Meanwhile, at night, the hallways of America clamor for justice, for reasonable rents, for the pipes not to freeze again please, and for a sale, any sale, on something necessary, and vital. Please? The angels are busy. Go to sleep.

In Fort Greene Park, on the hill, the big one, home of the Canarsee people until Joris Jansen Rapelje "bought" the area in 1637 and then General Nathanael Greene built Fort Putnam during the revolutionary war which was eventually torn down and turned into Fort Greene Park, the hill that my mom (who went to Pratt in the '70s) once told me they'd roll bodies down in the '70s, on *that hill*, at this instant, a bunch of kids were playing hide and seek. They hid in the trees, and behind benches, and three of them were behind Sam and Eleanor, they were laughing, nobody would ever find them there, their teachers were off in the distance, laughing, in the noon sun. Then a van rolled up to the park and a hundred cops poured out of it, swarming the kids. The cops yelled at them to STOP and opened fire, the kids fell dead left and right, meanwhile the teachers started screaming, and then the cops threw all the bodies into their van, and drove off, and nobody ever heard from those kids again. The sky was full of clouds that day, and, out in America, everyone's lives were basically still ahead of them, there was nothing more romantic than a high school gym with a band in it in a major motion picture, with a spotlight somewhere closing in on love, and everything around you is just violent yearning.

Oh my God when was the last time we watered the plants?

OK so it's 1861. This guy Allan Pinkerton claims he stopped someone from assassinating the President, and the President hires him to do his personal security during the Civil War, which was a very dramatic thing that happened when the South said WE WILL FUCKING KILL YOU IF WE CAN'T OWN PEOPLE FUCK YOU WE CAN TOTALLY OWN PEOPLE THEY AREN'T EVEN PEOPLE THEY ARE BLACKS BLACKS AREN'T PEOPLE and then the South tried to burn America to the ground, which is why racists carry around Confederate flags because I guess it's

easier than wearing a hood and setting a cross on fire to burn
Christ to death for commanding you to love with an open
heart, or whatever. People like to say the President wanted to
end slavery, but it seems pretty clear that by today's definition
he was not an abolitionist but a reformer, and anyway, he was
quoted as saying, "I will say then that I am not, nor ever have
been, in favor of bringing about in any way the social and
political equality of the white and black races," and the Thir-
teenth Amendment did end slavery, except "as a punishment
for crime whereof the party shall have been duly convicted,
shall exist within the United States, or any place subject to
their jurisdiction," which might go a long way towards ex-
plaining why it is that America has over two million people
in prison, why it has privatized prisons for profit, why it is
that prisoners are not allowed to vote but ARE counted in the
census, thus incentivizing cities and states to build more prisons so that they can have more representatives thanks to the
prisoners who cannot vote, and also the labor. Anyway, the
South fucking lost. OK, so eventually businesses decided that
what's good for the President is good for business and they began hiring the Pinkertons to infiltrate and destroy unions, and
they did! It worked out so well that, in 1871, Congress wanted
the Department of Justice to start a national detective agency,
but instead they just contracted it out to the Pinkertons, a private agency that also worked for the government, sort of like
when the government hires private mercenaries to go murder
people overseas, or in Mexico, or downtown, or wherever.
Eventually there was some trouble involving the Pinkertons
being used to murder workers, and in 1893, as his last act as
President, the President passed the Anti-Pinkerton Act, which,
despite what it sounds like, just meant that Pinkertons could

no longer be employed by the United States government, and then the next President had to send in the army to go murder the striking Pullman Company workers since they couldn't just hire it out to the Pinkertons now and "Sam," says Eleanor, "This isn't fun. This is just a history lesson, Sam, and I asked for a story. Why are you just lecturing? Lecturing is not an attractive trait, Sam." It isn't! But the thing is, the Pinkertons were used to crush, murder, defame, and destroy unions. Now, unions have done some dumb, corrupt, and horrific fucking things. But the point of unions is to give bargaining power to the worker. And that's good, right? It's good that you have a forty-hour workweek and that there's a minimum amount of money you can be paid for your labor, and yeah, it should be higher, but that's just because instead of hiring assholes with guns to fuck you over, ownership hires your representatives to fuck you over. This is America. It has so many promises! I cannot even keep them straight! I promise next time I'll be funnier. I swear to God.

Meanwhile, Sam wrote five new emails regarding payment for invoices he had indeed submitted but had reattached just in case. Sam has, at times, retained almost none of the revelations he has borne witness to. One check appeared, on time, like a miracle. Sam proofread four articles and six micro-reviews. Sam noticed all the pieces on nuclear assaults were no longer in the queue. Sam in fact could not remember anyone talking about this for at least a day. He texted Eleanor, *wasn't there gonna be a nuclear strike?* And Eleanor texted back, *lmao,* and sent a selfie with a hazy golden filter where her lips were somehow incredibly red and her eyes, which were blue like the ocean is blue, in that you absolutely always believe they're blue no matter what you actually see, and could also stare at them for hours, looked the bluest they'd ever looked. She had a halo. Sam smiled. Sam took his hand and ran it, slowly, down his whole face. He drank the coldest water the taps would give him. He put glass after glass of it in the fridge. Sam would never go thirsty. So many things in this world would happen before Sam went thirsty. Sam might even get paid before he went thirsty. The sun would go cold and the world would go dark before Sam went thirsty. Sam would get a salaried fucking job before he went thirsty, he would make Eleanor proud before he went thirsty, he would show her the sort of life her sort of kindness should yield with a house and a yard and whatever else it took to make her feel safe and know she was loved before he went thirsty. It would stop snowing before Sam went thirsty.

Meanwhile, the rubber tree plant had six leaves and ten branches at this point, and everyone was really very excited about this. Progress and growth will soon be upon us all, and we will be bathed in such grace as you could not dare imagine. Sam and Eleanor immediately sent out for a banner and a trophy. Your invitation to the party is in the mail, so clear your schedule.

Meanwhile the Pinkerton Detective Agency, those spineless cowards with guns waging war on the working class with every breath they take, still exist, as a division of Securitas AB,

a Swedish security company. In the morning, the President
makes an announcement on the radio about the secret police.
What are the secret police? I'm so glad you asked!

The secret police are just like regular police, except secret.
For whatever reason, people don't trust the police like they
used to, and so the President decided that if there were cops
who nobody knew were cops, like your neighbors, or that
woman at the bar, or the old guy feeding pigeons, why, those
cops could keep an eye on everyone! And also, since they're
secret, everything they did would be secret, and wouldn't
that be better? If we just didn't know what cops were up
to? Meanwhile, in the White House, the Press Secretary was
taking questions from the press. The room seemed alive, in a
bad way, and everyone was yelling. The Press Secretary said
Yes and the reporter said OK and asked a question about
the secret police, about how this was unconstitutional and
un-American and also illegal, and the Press Secretary said
what are you talking about? And the reporter repeated herself, and the Press Secretary's eyes went wide. The whole
press room stands up and puts the reporter in a black bag,
on a live radio broadcast, and they drag the bag out of the
room. Nobody says anything. It is absolutely silent. The nation is holding its breath. The Press Secretary apologizes to
everyone, and to the nation especially. The Press Secretary
thanks the secret police for their swift response to that horrific event. I'm sure we all feel a lot safer with the secret
police out here watching out for us, said the Press Secretary.
Thanks everyone, I hope you have a great day!

Eleanor's at work, where she designs websites, texting Sam about the secret police. I'd tell you what they were talking about, but there are so many people in need of websites and there simply isn't the time! Business is going so well that they hire a new boss. Eleanor's new boss, who looks exactly like her old boss, who has absolutely not one single thing about her that would make her different from her old boss (all available clues point to her being the old boss with a new title, we're waiting on results from the lab, I'll get back to you as soon as the lab gets back to me, I promise), takes Eleanor aside! "We can gut them," she tells Eleanor. "Every last one of them." Eleanor imagines a life on the corporate seas, side by side with her mentor, this newly titled stranger, who has just appointed herself Eleanor's mentor. "Do you want to see my business card?" the woman asks. Eleanor has a nodule on her thyroid. Once a year she gets a sonogram and a needle aspiration. In a few months, this, too, will be considered a preexisting condition, and she will, quite possibly, lose health care coverage. She wonders if Sam can get freelancer's insurance, and if this could cover her if they were domestic partners. Eleanor begins to search the internet, furiously, for several things at once. She makes eighteen websites. Her newly appointed mentor changes the color schemes and removes a widget, then adds two more, which do absolutely nothing. Eleanor texts Sam the page and the login and asks him if it works on his phone. It does! In the meantime, productivity is up. The waters are rising. This is what the woman tells Eleanor, over private chat. In two weeks, the office will be under water, and she'll sail the corporate seas for a new office of a similar or greater height. Across the street, a mother walks out the door with a daughter and into a black bag and nobody ever sees them ever again. They built those bags so that they could swallow up the past and the present and the future all at once. Nothing would ever come out of those bags ever again. It was really something, when you thought about it.

This is fucked, thinks Eleanor. What is fucked? The future? Probably! But right now Eleanor is thinking about work. Eleanor likes her job. She's good at it, and it pays well, and she gets decent tax breaks, and there are good incentives, and they pay for her MetroCard without taking it out of her check, and there are free ball games she can take Sam to because Sam fucking loves ball games, and she fucking loves Sam. The world is a sustainable place while she works. *In two weeks*, the woman chats her, *Under water*. Eleanor screenshots this and sends it to Sam. She hits unsend. God bless the unsend button and all its minor salvations. *Dear God*, prays Eleanor, *First off, thank you for the unsend button and all its minor salvations. Really, it's amazing. I know it's been a while, but here's the deal. I've been blessed with a good job and love in my life. I make enough money to not be scared of a bill anymore and to try to help others with what's left over and maybe once in a while take a vacation. And that's all I fucking want, God! And Sam! Sam's a good cook and his dick's not scary and he's kind. And anyway, I don't know what to do here, God. The world's full of people for whom wanting'll never be enough because they'll just want more because they can because when they grew up their parents told them they could have whatever they wanted if they just worked hard enough and what they wanted was everything and so they took it, and these people, they're gonna fuck us all into this corporate police state where we all get blackbagged to a basement and they take our lives and then they take all the stuff we got and we don't get any say because all we wanted was just enough money to not be scared of a bill, and it turns out that was the wrong thing to want. I don't get it. Or, I don't want to get it, God. I really really don't. I don't believe in Heaven because it's an idea invented to keep the poor working their asses off for nothing at all but the promise that when they die, it'll all have been worth it. I can't believe that that's what you wanted here. I'm not asking for a sign, God. But if you felt compelled, I wouldn't be upset about it. You know? Anyway. Amen.* She pricks her finger to make some sort of sign in blood but remembers that she has no idea how Jews wrap up their prayers, and now she feels like a shitty Jew, when all she wanted was to beseech God for a sign. She pushes the pushpin back in the drawing Sam made her that says *sadness!* in cursive on a banner on a heart cocked to the side. She smiles a bit. Lightning crashes, or the server does. Everyone is sent home early. The trains are delayed.

When Sam and Eleanor were younger, they absolutely hated "This Land Is Your Land." They thought it was fucking corny, and it is!, assuming you skip the last three verses, which say "As I went walking I saw a sign there, and on the sign it said 'No Trespassing.' But on the other side it didn't say nothing. That side was made for you and me. In the shadow of the steeple I saw my people, by the relief office I seen my people;

as they stood there hungry, I stood there asking *Is this land made for you and me?* Nobody living can ever stop me, as I go walking that freedom highway; nobody living can ever make me turn back, this land was made for you and me." "This Land Is Your Land" is such a good fucking song, and if you skip those verses, then you're the reason Woody Guthrie wrote this song. To skip these verses is to tell the story of America wherein America was not a nation built on, and codified by, genocide and theft. If you skip those verses you're the reason we forget that Hitler built the Nazi party from the lessons he learned from Jim Crow, you're the reason we don't care that Henry Ford was awarded the Grand Cross of the German Eagle, the highest medal the Nazis could give a foreigner, you're the reason it's hard to find out exactly how much money Henry Ford gave the Nazis, you're the reason we forget that every Ford was sold with a copy of the *Dearborn Independent* in the front seat, a paper Ford purchased in order to spread anti-Semitism as far and as wide as he could, you're why we don't talk about how he was building tanks for the Nazis while investing in campaigns to keep America out of the war and refusing to produce anything for the American war effort until at least 1942, earning him the comment that Ford helped to serve as an arsenal of Nazism by the US Army in 1945 (sorry, anti-Semitism is on my mind these days, I don't know why), you're why we don't care that the CIA trained the mujahideen who became Al-Qaeda, or that we trained and installed Saddam Hussein. And, I know, I know it's been said before, and by better people than me, but, this is America. This land is neither your land, nor my land. This land belongs to the dead. OK so it's 1932. The renegade cowboy and columnist Will Rogers invents trickle-down economics as a joke about the worst thing you could ever do to a person. America misunderstands him like it misunderstands all renegade cowboys and promptly begins to burn itself to the ground.

That's it! That's all I have to say about that!

This evening, Sam and Eleanor will move the rubber tree plant onto an antique wooden folding chair with a sheepskin rug from Eleanor's dead grandmother slung over the back and place it directly in front of the window. This will show them. This will show them all.

Sam is in the grocery store getting ready to make dinner. Sam gets some haricot vert and a lemon and some Yukon golds and a real big rib eye, which he has to think about for a minute, about buying it, but he figures fuck it, death comes for us all. Sam goes home and begins boiling the potatoes and browning some butter and tossing some garlic, not too much garlic, for once, in that wonderfully browning butter right before it browns so that nothing burns and everything's wonderful, he puts a grill pan on the stove, he mashes the potatoes and mixes in the browned butter and garlic and some buttermilk and some mayo and salt and pepper and a little bit of thyme. Anyway in the grocery store, earlier, this woman came in, on a horse, in full riding gear, and she trampled a baby, spilling its brains and blood and screams all over the inexcusable linoleum, the baby's father's rending his garments, his tears flooding the floor and carrying his dead son on home, the lights in the store growing brighter and brighter and brighter and brighter, as the lady on the horse bought some Count Chocula, paid cash, and then left. It was at this point that Sam decided to get the rib eye.

Jane's boss asks her to stay late. Jane's boss comes into the office with a bottle of scotch and a hat, I shit you not, hanging off his erect cock. Jane takes a photo and sends it to HR. Jane is offered a transfer to another office. Jane goes home and she sits in her room and she wonders what it would be like to move to Cleveland and buy a house and live in a city where she could watch live baseball and where she didn't know a single fucking soul. What would that feel like? To be alone in a city of strangers? How different would it be from now, and is that a crown on your head? Is it on fire? Is there a chorus in faint accompaniment, and can you taste grace, and if so, would you describe it? Please? It was raining in Cleveland in her mind. The Tigers were delayed. Jane was listening on the radio. She was imagining a life. It was a specific life. *I'd like*, she texted Johnny, but the texts went from blue to green. Jane scrolled up. *I'm sorry I just can't keep doing this*, said Johnny, at 3:30 this morning. Did you ever wonder why we use the term *break*? Does it matter if everyone has had the same thought? Does a revelation contain less grace if it's not yours alone? In Cleveland, Jane imagines, play resumed. It always does. In Queens, an entire subway car was put in an unmarked police van and taken to an undisclosed location. In Cleveland, Jane imagines, the Tigers won. The Cuyahoga burst into flames and drowned the whole city. The Mayor petitioned Heaven for an angel. The city waits.

When the angels come,
all your money will
burn and burn and burn.

IT'S STILL WINTER. It's still snowing. A truly fascinating economy involving shoveling and landlords has sprung up throughout the city. Crews of children roam the streets with shovels bigger than their bodies and forearms to match. This, like so many American inventions, can only end well.

Come morning, our phones start screaming for us to wake up, please, please just wake up. Please! Today Eleanor got up first. She'd been sleeping pretty well since everyone stopped talking about a nuclear strike on New York City every fucking day! Sam, though, Sam'd had trouble sleeping again. Eleanor got dressed. She tried to be quiet. She left a note for Sam. He just had to push the button.

Something that Sam and Eleanor had learned over their years of sleeping together was important to note here, and it was this: Sam had always been a bad sleeper, and Eleanor had always been a good sleeper, and only one of them was ever allowed to get a good night's sleep at a time. If you were wondering who wrote that rule, I really don't know, I wish I did, I have several words I would like to have with them, and only one of those words is a kind one.

The snow is weeping. The postal workers walking through the snow, the sleet, the dead of night, are weeping. The dead of night is weeping and so are the dead. The dead are still weeping. This is America. The dead weep in America. All across America, the sleeping Americans are weeping. Even their tears are weeping! Sam's debt is weeping and Eleanor in her sleep is weeping from thinking about Sam's debt, which is weeping, and the weight it places upon his future every single day and Sam's future is weeping and weeping and weeping and we are, I swear to God, drowning our dreams in the weeping. This has been the weeping report. Tune in next time for more weeping.

The other night Sam and Eleanor got into bed and they watched part of a movie, the one where, in order for the angels to finally come, they have to give up their immortality and their direct link to the divine, but in return they get to see colors and taste stuff and fall in love and die. Eleanor fell asleep before the angels came and Sam finished the movie, turning down the volume on the laptop so as not to wake her, letting her hold onto him as she kicked off down into sleep, Sam closed the movie at its end before closing the laptop as near total darkness swallowed the room and Sam took a breath, slowly, and, releasing it, had a drink of water, put lotion on his hands, lay back down, closed his eyes which he was too tired to keep open, maybe this time it'll be different, maybe this time Sam'll fall asleep. Meanwhile the trains were still, more or less, running. Meanwhile the moon went to bed. Meanwhile the sun rose somewhere as Eleanor showered and dressed and got on the train. Snow was still falling. She emailed work to say she would be late, and so did everyone else.

Last night, in the Bronx, while Yankee Stadium was in the midst of its winter-long nap, at a subway station, anyone who didn't have their birth certificate in their pocket got hand-cuffed and blackbagged and thrown into a moving train and nobody ever saw them ever again. The snow fell. That was all. The other week Eleanor got Sam a video game where he could finally be there when the angels come, if he wanted to. It was the nicest thing she could think of that day. Today Sam had no deadlines, because he had no work. No work had come in down the pipeline of late and really any way you looked at it, things could be better for Sam. Which is why Eleanor got Sam a video game where he could be there when the angels come, finally, if he wanted to. She had been at work, thinking about Sam, and she'd seen some reviews for this game, and none of them made any sense. But, basically, you could be there for the moment when the angels come.

In the game, you're an angel! You're a wingéd shimmering column of light with a billion eyes and a flaming sword. Sam walks around Heaven. It's full of angels. Sam packs into a closet with all of them. All of the angels. The room smells like burning feathers and light. I mean the room Sam is in, in his apartment. Don't ask me to explain it, I don't have the educa-tion to make sense of this. As an angel, you can fly around Heaven. As an angel, you can fly around Earth. There aren't any instructions, there isn't a tutorial, and the internet itself is just as confused. Sam, for a while, cannot remember if the button for bringing down his flaming sword of judgment is X or if it's O. One of the buttons is for bringing down the flam-ing sword of judgment, God's divine wrath, and the other is for listening to the thoughts and dreams of the people here on Earth. Sam feels absolutely terrible as he brings down his flaming sword of judgment, God's divine wrath, on people whose faces he tries to forget, people he wanted so badly to listen to, to help. You can help! You can guide people onto a path of light. You can save their souls from torment. In the game, torment is suffering as it is here on Earth. It's starvation, it's rape, it's the police, it's hunger, it's never having enough money, enough food, it's a hole in the roof or your arm. Torment is real, and it surrounds us. You can put money in people's wallets, in their accounts, you can bring down your flaming sword of judgment, God's divine wrath, on the cops as they shoot children in their own front yards. You can just watch. You can watch everything. All around are the angels.

So yeah, sometimes all the angels, I mean every single angel in Heaven, had to walk into the closet of the smallest bedroom in the fifth-biggest apartment in Heaven, which rotated, and you had to be holding your flaming sword, and you had to find a way to get in that closet, with all the other angels, there were thousands of them, packed into this incredibly small closet, with their flaming swords, and sometimes this smell would fill the air like maybe burning feathers and a blinding white light, it was weird, no one knew where the smell came from, it was a simple button combination to find the right way to get in there and you had to actually move around a little to avoid singeing the wings of the other angels, it was a little meditative, and sometimes, in the game, you were flying around, watching a child's first steps, a balloon lost in the sky, following it all the way up, maybe you bear witness to centuries of death and pain and then everything gets topsy-turvy at the office, you have to sit down, because of all the death and pain, and then you think maybe you can walk away from it all, trade in your wings for this sack of skin, get a job, go to work, live a life, and die, apparently it's the only way to get the story to end, otherwise you just keep on going, every day, Eleanor'd even heard once someone got the angels to unionize, attempted to redistribute the glory of Heaven on Earth, anyway, Eleanor had been thinking, fondly, on the train, and with a little sadness, about Sam, while Sam, at this very moment, in bed, grabbed his phone, opened his eyes, and found there was still no work. He wrote four emails. He checked in with one website that had not yet paid for copy Sam wrote six to eight business weeks ago. The other three were to follow up on things that either did or did not need to be followed up on, showing he was thorough, and attentive, and then he went and showered the desperation off in the shower as he ran through his day, and weighed his decisions. He mapped out events. He formulated a plan. He stood on the ledge of a building and leapt. He was a column of light with a billion eyes. His wings spread wider and wider and he kept falling, faster and faster and faster, the spat-on street rising up to greet him, and he was through it, he was in a subway car, he was moving, all around him were the people, he was with them all. Have you ever looked at a subway car in the morning? Of course you have. What am I talking about? Have you ever looked at a subway car full of people whose hearts you could hear as words in a video game after not having any financial stability in your life for four years? Have you ever sometimes forgotten about the wonder that is present in the world? Have you ever confused the button for nudging someone towards a path of redemption and light with the button for bringing down your flaming sword of judgment, God's divine wrath? Of course not, right? Who would do that? A thing like that! Well. His heart in disarray, Sam went to make coffee. He saw Eleanor's note and pushed the button. Then there was coffee. Eleanor got it all ready, he just had to push the button. *I love you so much*, thought Sam.

Sam sat at the table in the room where they did all their living, with his coffee, which was absolutely hot, and perfect, and he thought about all the things we can do for the people who love us, and the clouds parted, and he was bathed in light, and he wept.

Meanwhile Eleanor was still on the subway. She was still reading that book about the end of the world. It turns out that the end of the world is going to be a problem. (It also turns out the world has ended several times already, and what'll happen is that all of humanity'll be wiped out, and we'll all die and so will our children and our money, and then one day something else will rise up and find reasons to make other people's lives worse and worse and worse for the sake of a nicer vacation, etc., forever, amen.) They have started to bring in dogs into the office, soft dogs with kind eyes, for emotional support, they are keeping them in a pen full of toys in a room full of sad lighting to make everyone feel better, in winter, which is endless, as means of combatting this now months-long war waged against the sun. Meanwhile Sam had a slice of key lime pie from the other night. The other night, there was key lime pie. It was salted, and delicious, and I cannot believe I forgot to tell you about it. Two hours after she'd first left the apartment, Eleanor got off the train and walked to her office. The sky was cold.

Up in Heaven are the angels. In Heaven, they're just pillars of shimmering light with a million eyes and indescribable wings and their flaming sword of judgment, God's divine wrath. In Heaven, they're beautiful. Up in Heaven, there's a party. A thing you should maybe know about angels is that angels can't taste anything, and they don't have a single thing between their legs, and it isn't that they can't see colors so much as it is that, as pillars of shimmering light, the world just washes over them, all the time, forever. And then later some of the angels got to talking and they said, well, you know, we haven't, up in Heaven, seen a good war in a while, in honestly so long they'd almost forgotten, having been alive for the entirety of existence, having only really been to war that one time, in a sort of civil war, which nobody really likes to talk about, family all dead, all of them dead, which, yknow, things get a little wobbly then, but, BUT! Sam, in Heaven, with the angels, in his video game, did not like how this conversation was going! So he left! The kingdom of Heaven is a weird sad place, just brimming with light. It is everywhere at once. And they can see you. The gangs of shoveling children and their massive forearms have been approached by organizers. They have begun to organize. The landlords, looking out upon their eternal city, begin to sweat. Somewhere, out there, are the secret police. You can never forget about the secret police. OK?

Nobody ever forgets about the secret police because as soon as you forget about the secret police, the secret police walk out of the closet they made of your mouth and they walk you into a black bag for the rest of your life and after that you can never forget about them ever again and then after that you'll be dead.

As Eleanor steps out of the subway, her phone floods with texts Sam sent during her two-hour commute underground. She'll notice the texts when she gets to her desk and takes her phone out of her bag. The light doesn't really change from the stairwell to the street. There are times in winter where you have no idea where you are. The light never changes except when it goes to sleep at completely unreasonable hours, like, say, 4:00 p.m. on a Friday. Once upon a time there was this song that basically said this world is not my home I'm just a-passin through, and while it was about Heaven, which is a lie rich people invented so poor people would find glory in their own personal suffering, there are whole days where it's still a sentiment you can really get behind.

Did it change your life? Did the angels come? Did the world end? Was it all better? For once? Well?
    Well?

Eleanor drops her bag under her desk and boots up her computer. Her monitor blinks its way to life. She flinches at the monitor and walks over to get coffee. When she comes back, her inbox will start to yell at her, which is fun, it is a fun thing when your inbox yells at you, let me tell you, she tells Sam, who thinks, but does not mention, how much less fun it is when your inbox stares out at you like what philosophers have referred to as *the abyss*. Sam moves through the city and the city moves through Sam. Meanwhile, people are saying the trains are going to be canceled all weekend while they shovel out the tunnels. Does this mean Eleanor lives here now? Isn't this when the angels are supposed to come? Now, in our hour of need? It is just such a balm, in troubled times, like these, to have questions! Meanwhile, it's Friday. It's easily past time for lunch. Somewhere in America everything is fine and we wish you could be there to see it. Meanwhile Eleanor's computer screen passes her a note that her direct report is being let go. To her left is a door. Someone has brought dogs to the office. She is checking the margins for the data we all missed. She is drawing up fifteen wireframes, and no one will like any of them. She could make the wireframes they'd like. She has a file. It's the same file every time. That's what they want. Maybe with some flash before the browsers all reject it. And something cute, and responsive. But then she'd just sit in the office all day with virtually nothing to do. And then she'd try to think about practical solutions to income inequality in America, and that is an overwhelming thing to fucking think about! While this was happening, Sam got up and made lunch. He cut up an apple. He put a real tiny bit of olive oil in the pan and put a big pat of butter in the olive oil, and sprinkled grated cheddar and jack from a zippable sack onto some bread with a little parmesan which he then placed in the pan, where the butter was hot. Now he flips it to make sure it's been evenly browned and the cheese is melted. He sprinkles it with some kosher salt. He eats his lunch, and it's wonderful. He's a column of light, with a billion eyes, and a pair of the most beautiful wings. He holds aloft his flaming sword. In the game, he sees someone in an office who looks exactly like Eleanor. The room across from her is filling with dogs. They've reached the ceiling now. They're barking but there isn't any sound. The person who looks like Eleanor is sitting at her computer. It looks like she's doing everything she can to not look directly at the dogs.

Sam is standing next to her. He is looking right at the dogs. The dogs will not look at him. Sam looks at the dogs. There's a sound, but he can't quite tell what it is. Sam gets up and looks out the window. The youths are shoveling, and people have called the cops. The cops pull their guns. The kids dive into the snowbanks. Nobody will find them for hours. The cops don't know what to do. Their sirens are moving, but they're silent. It isn't that. Sam sits back down. The dogs have seen him, now. The sound is everywhere.

Eleanor checks the trains. They are canceled. The trains are dead! Everyone's monitors slip them a note and the note it says THE TRAINS ARE CANCELED! IT WILL BE A FUN WORK WEEKEND! YAY!!! Eleanor's heart falls all the way through her. She will never leave this place. She will die here. Maybe Sam can fly here and save her. She texts Sam, *The trains are dead please fly here and save me?* Eleanor looks at pictures of Sam as a child on her phone. His hair is so blond. His smile nearly eats his face. You can watch his dimple grow up. Her heart swells. The dogs finally notice her. They lose their minds.

One day, not today, but one day, we will be glory-bound. We will be washed in His blood, at sunset, with the rest of our lives ahead of us, and everything will be full of promise, and beauty. Meanwhile! The secret police are at your door. They're dressed up as the seats on the subway. They're packed into your cupboards. They line the aisles of the Associated Market. They're hiding inside the fingers of the little boy touching every piece of bread in the grocery store. They are everywhere, and they are waiting, just for you.

Sam's phone tells Sam that Eleanor is telling Sam that the trains are canceled, and that she is stuck at work all weekend. Sam pauses the game. He stands by the window. "Jesus," he says. "Yeah," she says. Eleanor is nowhere near the dogs right now. "Somehow there is catering. En route. Apparently there is a room with bunk beds. This building is a mystery." Sam tells her to beware strange rooms, and the things inside them. "Please come home," he says. "I am trying!" says Eleanor, as though Sam was saying she was not trying! Sam is not saying that, though. He tells her he loves her. "I love you," he says. "When you come home, there will be dinner, no matter the hour, and it'll be warm, and it'll warm you. You can take a hot bath. I'll boil the water in pots if I have to. It'll be as nice as it can be. I swear to God." "O God what if the pipes freeze?" asks Eleanor. Sam tells her they won't. He tells her the building is too big, it used to be a hospital, the pipes are incredibly well insulated. Eleanor is thinking about Sam's old apartment. The bathroom's pipes ran down into this open passageway by the outdoor trash tunnel. Every winter they'd freeze. Sam and Geronimo, his roommate, would fill buckets with water from the kitchen sink, whose pipes did *not* freeze, to put in the toilet so it would flush. Once, back then, Sam came over to Eleanor's to shower, in total awe of her bathroom, which was almost the exact same size as the rest of the apartment, which was small for an apartment, and enormous for a bathroom, and also the fixtures were gilded, it was really something to write home about, which they both did, on more than one occasion. They'd just started dating. "I'm coming home, Sam. One day. I don't know when. But I'm coming home. I swear to God, Sam." "I know. I love you. Be wary of strange rooms and mysterious animals brought in for unfamiliar purposes." Eleanor hung up. She looked out the window.

The thing about war is that there was always one going at one point or another and we knew that the death tolls were high and rising ever higher with each consecutive administration, like so many other costs of living, and if we'd learned anything at all from the movies it was of the great red swath cutting its way across the map of history.

This one time, a member of the secret police got lost in the Soviet-Bloc-style tunnels in the basement of Sam and Eleanor's building. Sam came across the secret policeman, weeks later, emptying a long-empty clip into a wall while hissing through cracked-open lips *shh! shh! shh!!* black bags piled up around the secret policeman like a horrible snowdrift in the corner, and Sam hit them over the head with a fire extinguisher and went upstairs and posted on the building's message board *hi every-one, saw something weird in the basement, looks like a fire ex-tinguisher fell onto someone's head, seemed like they'd been there for a while, just wanted to give everyone a heads up* and then Sam logged off the message board and never logged on again.

I don't really know how to tell you about this. But I'd like to. I'd like to tell you once about this dream I had. We were just bathed in light. The whole world had fallen away and there was nothing that could stand between us, nothing but light, and the light just got bigger and bigger and bigger and bigger and bigger and bigger and bigger and bigger and bigger and bigger and bigger and bigger and bigger and bigger and big-ger and bigger and bigger and bigger and then I woke up and there you were. I keep trying to find ways to say this so that it feels as important as I seem to think it is. And anyway it is probably time to change the subject, because the catering has arrived! It is an early dinner! There will be midnight snacks! There are dogs! Everything is nice! Isn't this nice?

Sam's been weird lately, is something Eleanor's noticed. He hasn't been himself. He puts everything he has into dinner, ev-ery spare thought, as though it's the one thing he can do right for Eleanor, and it breaks her heart. It's incredibly hard to feel worthless. It's just a hard thing to do. And it's really fucking hard to be that person's fucking partner! I mean thank God for the dinners! But, Jesus, baby, you wonder on Earth, you being of light, just open your heart back up to love, please, for all of our sakes?

Eleanor brings her open-faced chicken parm on focaccia to her desk. She has a cup full of a cold salad of steamed broccoli, garlic, and white wine vinegar. She idly stabs it with a fork. Outside the snow is falling.

Eleanor's computer slips her a note that says ten people have just been fired. She stands up from the dogs, who have surrounded her and are visibly upset by the lack of attention, and she tries to do a head count. The dogs bark. Their barks grow louder and louder and louder. They drown out the office. Eleanor blinks once, blinks twice. Then it stops.

Sam sees something weird, down below. He goes on down. There's a weird door. Sam knows he could open it. He could walk through it. Sam could walk through that door, into a new life. If that was a thing he wanted.

Eleanor's in a meeting where some things no one seems to be able to recall are said and after the meeting they are shown the bunk beds. They are nicer than you'd think, honestly. It's incredibly nice and it manages to seem private and feel safe while also generating a sort of summer camp atmosphere. Nobody can leave the building.

Sam goes to bed. He forgot to light the candles. In the middle of the night, he rolls over to hold onto Eleanor. He blinks.

In the morning, Eleanor's boss calls her in for breakfast. There are omelets. Eleanor loves omelets. "It's you and me, kid," her boss says. Eleanor has no idea how old this woman is. Online, her profiles vary. "How did you sleep?" "I missed Sam, it was strange, I—" "Pretty great we got those bunks set up, right? I found them to be genuinely intimate while still allowing one to maintain a sense of privacy." Eleanor could see a California king under the desk. It smelled new. There was a California king–sized mountain of plastic in the corner. The world was absolutely getting stranger every day. "Kid, it is you, and it is me." This was true, in that everyone else was fired. Once people were fired, they were no longer in the building. It seemed like something that was best not think about too much. The dogs have started to bark. They are outside the glass office, and barking. No sound comes out. Eleanor feels like the world is not, at the moment, making sense. "What is happening," asks Eleanor, dazed from the barking, from sleeping in a bunk bed, from not leaving work, unable to swallow the question, a small way in which our emails have bested us. The dogs are showing their teeth now. You should too.

Eleanor just sits at her desk. The dogs bark. They fill the room.

One hundred and seventy-five people have been blackbagged by the secret police—who are secret, and who are waiting, just for you—in America since Eleanor went to work yesterday. Nobody will ever see them again, and nobody, not even their mothers, will remember their names by the end of this.

On the one hand, 175 people is a lot of people, and on the other hand, you might be dead inside. Once upon a time I used to want a Viking funeral. Wouldn't that be beautiful?

Say Eleanor can't ever come home. Say the snow never stops and, instead, it rises a floor a month, packed so tight and deep that the only way out is to make a fire out of the whole floor so the windows burst open and you jump out onto the snow. Say people try this and promise to get help. Say help never comes. Say Eleanor becomes mayor of the building within a decade. One day she wakes up. She is clad in the furs of her enemies, who are numerous, and unreasonable. The city is silent. She walks out the door. Everything is quiet. Even the wind is holding its breath. Sam has been dead for years. In the freezer is a dinner, just for her. It's been waiting all this time.

I love you so much. Can you tell yet?

It isn't good that Eleanor's gone, and it isn't good that Sam doesn't have any work, but!, this *is* a perfect time for Sam to lose hours of his life to trying to understand what happens when the angels come. The game has no plot, and the only way to get a game over, again, is to become human, removing your beautiful wings, your flaming sword of judgment, God's divine wrath, your billion eyes, renounce your existence as a shimming column of light, get up, go to work, fall in love, and then die. Sam has not done this. You can find people in the game. I mean like real people. Sam has found Eleanor, and he has found his parents. He has found the President and the Mayor and the landlords and the union organizers, and he has protected the gangs of youths with shovels from the secret police, who are everywhere. The story he has seen on message boards on the internet is that when you renounce your existence as an angel you go out into the world and live your life. *Your* life. You can make every choice you have ever made, but you can only make it once. Once you're not an angel, there isn't a save option, and you can't restart. That's it. Your existence as an extension of the divine is endless and eternal, your life as a human is a straight line to death. It's just so beautiful.

The gang of youths woke up and shoveled the walks of the city. Their negotiators have met with the landlords and come to an agreement. For now, there is a sort of peace in Brooklyn. The sun is up. The snow is a solemn miracle in this light. Let's just see what happens next.

Please.

Again, I want you to imagine that you haven't had a stable income in years. I want you to feel like you exist by the grace of the love of others. I want you to imagine that there is no clear path out of this, and I want you to think that that can't be possible, and I want you to look at the job market, and what being a freelancer entails, and I want you to apply for jobs you're overqualified for and not get them because you're overqualified for them, and I want you to apply for jobs you are qualified for, but so is everyone else, and the jobs you could get don't pay enough, and you can't get them because they think you're overqualified, and I want you to look at how your $70,000 student loan is now about $140,000 eight years later, even though you have never missed a payment, even when you were on assistance for several months, I want you to sit with all of that, and then I want a video game to show up, in your lap, on a weekend when you are completely alone, and the video game is about a world you have always wanted to think about. I just want you to try to hold all of that in your head right now. OK? Thanks!

At Eleanor's work, a hot bar has been set up for a working brunch. There is mac and cheese, and a sort of tofu dish with broth and hot peppers, and a salad with kale and pears and sliced almonds and a sesame dressing, and some sort of chicken that maybe was even grilled, and an omelet bar. It all smells great, and there is enough for everyone, isn't that convenient? There will be a meeting later! It will be incredibly informative. Meanwhile, in the game, Sam walked out the door into a bar. Sam was a pillar of light. There was this young couple there. All around them were the secret police. Sam misses Eleanor so much. He can't find her anywhere. The couple is talking about a dream they had. All around them were the secret police. Don't worry, this isn't the dream they had, this is just what's happening. The secret police were in the seats, and the tables, they were at the door, they were in the kitchen, they were waiting, they were everywhere. This is the part where Sam takes out his flaming sword of judgment, God's divine wrath, and the secret police die screaming. The young couple gets up. Sam puts a million dollars in the trunk of their car. Sam flies around New York City, killing the secret police. In the game, Sam goes around and gathers up money and redistributes it to people who are hungry. He goes around and builds homeless shelters into homes so people can have some homes and he builds them up high high into the sky so everyone can have a balcony. Sam is a pillar of light. He blinks once. Blinks twice. In her office, Eleanor is in the meeting. It's too late. She's trying to figure out how much of this is worth listening to. The lights are dim. There's a smell she can't place. Sam isn't answering her texts. "If we concentrate, it can all be ours. We can take it all. All of it. All that we can see!" This is the part where the angels come to Sam. Sam would give absolutely anything for Eleanor to come home. Eleanor feels stunned. She has been here for so long. Absolutely none of this matters, and it is consuming so much of her life, and it's entirely terrifying. She looks for someone she recognizes. Somebody says: "Isn't it exciting?" They are so very excited. It's incredibly jarring. Sam aches everywhere. He washes his hands. He gets up. He blinks. He turns the lights on. Everything looks different right now. His life settles in around him. He made a deal with the angels for Eleanor to come home. Eleanor looks up from her phone, at work, and finds herself looking up from her phone on the train, which is moving, and then someone throws up. Sam starts up the rice cooker and gathers up some eggs and some vegetables. There's an onion somewhere, and garlic, and some carrots, and a thing of broccoli he can cut up real small. There's a pork chop and a chicken breast in the freezer and some steak in a container in the fridge. Sam quickly thaws and chops the chicken and the pork chop and shoves them in a ziplock full of hoisin sauce to try to marinate. Sam chops up the vegetables and throws them in the wok with some bacon fat. Everyone in the train car retreats to the sides. The smell is inescapable. At the next stop everyone runs to another car while the incoming passengers boldly board the now-empty one. Four people get trapped by the closing doors. The closing doors were the secret police all along! Eleanor is standing next to a woman and her daughter as the mother is blackbagged by the secret police and the daughter is left standing there, holding onto a hand that's gone. Sam tosses the thawed and hurriedly marinated meat in the wok with some more bacon fat. He whisks some eggs with soy sauce and hot sauce. He fries it all with the rice. Eleanor walks in the door. Sam is running a bath. Eleanor could just weep right now. She could just completely break down into tears right now. Everything is fine, except for all the things you can't ever explain. Outside it's raining. It's freezing. The entire sky is weeping. It's nice. It's soothing. Just hold me a little longer, please.

Everything is good here.

Please come home.

WHEN I LOOK AT YOU standing in the doorway like that all rimmed with light like that as I walk up to you like that what happens is that it feels like I love you so much that I can't breathe. It feels like I love you so much that if I were to let you take my breath away like that then the world'd end right then and there. I think it's cute that we all always try to keep breathing. That we refuse, day in and day out, to let beauty take our breath away, to have the sky crack open for good and always. It's cute. It really is.

What's for dinner?

SAM'S GONNA MAKE SPAGHETTI AND MEATBALLS. "Tonight I'm going to make spaghetti and meatballs," he said. They've just woken up, and it's morning. Eleanor immediately called in sick, or worked from home, because tonight Sam's gonna make spaghetti and meatballs. Later, Sam dropped two heads of garlic and an onion into the food processor and put that into a pan with some oil. He grated a bunch of pecorino, I don't know how much, enough to fill most of a grater box, if that makes any sense. Sam uses pecorino now, but he's used parmesan and asiago before, so if you want to try it, it's absolutely your call. He soaked as many slices of bread as there were pounds of meat in oat milk, because of how Eleanor's insides felt about dairy (he couldn't skip the cheese, so this is the compromise). He gathered up one egg per pound of meat, and breadcrumbs, and salt, and pepper. He put a parmesan rind and some tomato sauce in the slow cooker. He turned it on. He mixed everything (first the salt and pepper and the eggs then the breadcrumbs then the garlic and onions cooked down in oil, some more salt and pepper, the bread soaked in milk, the cheese, some more salt and pepper, more bread-crumbs when it seems like it all just needs to hold together a little more) in with the ground beef and pork and veal. He shaped each meatball with his hands and dropped it into the sauce which was in a slow cooker and would cook like that for about three hours. Eleanor looked so tired. Sam drew her a bath until dinner was ready. Three hours later he started the pasta. Then dinner was ready. "This is really nice!" said Eleanor, while they drank a nice big fucking red. The whole world, that night, smelled like home.

Listen sometimes we just have to let things in the world be
nice. We just have to say *this is nice!* and mean it and then
everything is just nice. We have to just let it be *nice*. We have
to find a way to get through this. You know? It's either that or
we burn everything to the fucking ground. Those really seem
like the only choices sometimes!

Eleanor can't sleep. Why? Let's look at her thoughts! Maybe
they'll have the answer! *Could we solve income inequality
in America by telling the cops we saw income inequality in
America trying to break into a car and then the cops would
shoot income inequality in America in the face until it was
dead? Would that also work for climate change? Maybe the
secret police can come and deal with irreversible climate
change and just like, shoot it in the face. God I sound like
Sam. But also, just picture it: cops yell at climate change to
go back where it came from while shooting climate change in
the face, the secret police file out of vans and just blackbag
everything. The reputation of vans will never recover from
this. Just tell them to pretend climate change is a cute brown
six-year-old. Wow actually maybe if we told them climate
change was wearing a hoodie and looked suspicious they'd
do something about it. God. Is there even a point in staying employed when the world's going to end? And then you
know, you think, maybe you want a baby, and so then you
have a baby, and it's so beautiful, and you love it so much,
you hold this beautiful daughter to your skin, which is basically made of love, in this moment, which is endless, or
it seems endless, and she loves you so much, she looks you*

right in the eyes, and she smiles at you, and then she throws up all over you, and she looks you in the eye and says Why would you bring me into this world to die choking on hot poison air while a boiling sea drowns every dream I ever had? Why would you do that? I thought you were gonna protect me! I thought you loved me! And the baby is just screaming now I THOUGHT YOU LOVED ME I THOUGHT YOU LOVED ME I THOUGHT YOU LOVED ME. OH! *And then there are all those people out there who want the world to end so they can go up to heaven! Because this world doesn't matter and if we kill it, if we make sure the world ends, then we can go to heaven forever. So that's great. That's fun. And oh my god the dinner Sam made! I could kiss him on the dick! Then the angels would come. They wouldn't say anything. They'd just sort of float there, glowering in judgment, and molting all over these rented hardwood floors. Fuck the angels. Fuck them. Fuck. We could actually see the world end. Why are we doing anything other than trying to make sure the world doesn't end? Why?????????????????* Eleanor can't sleep. She turns over to Sam and says his name, "Sam," to try to wake him up. Sam is a shitty sleeper and needs all the sleep he can get. This doesn't matter right now, though. It's an extraneous detail, so don't worry about it. Someone needs to watch over their loved one's dreams. I'll say that much. Meanwhile Eleanor is saying "SAM" louder and louder. Sam rolls over onto her. This solves nothing. "This solves nothing," says Eleanor, while Sam lays flopped on top of her. She says, "Sam, I cannot sleep." Even if Sam could fall back asleep again, he could not do it if Eleanor was up, and upset, because he would feel terrible for her, because she loves to sleep, and it breaks his heart

when she's sad. It just breaks his fucking heart wide open! So
Sam gets up. Sam gets everyone a nice glass of ice-cold water.
Sam puts on an old cartoon where this clown goes into a mysterious cave while the snow falls and a beautiful woman is in
a glass coffin, and then a witch, flying on a mirror, puts her
mirror over the clown like a net and then the clown's a ghost,
he's in love, then everything's chilly, it's cold, it's frozen over,
there's nothing but the snow. They watch a cartoon where a
sad little ghost sits in a graveyard looking at pictures of animals till the other ghosts wake up, they try to get the sad little
ghost to go around and spook everyone, they're a bunch of
ghost planes in the sky, dive-bombing homes for miles around,
screaming BOO at everyone they hit, but the sad little ghost
sees no future in any pain beyond his own, and he goes out
to make friends, but everyone is terrified of him, due to him
confronting them with not only their own mortality, but the
possibility that Heaven is, if not a lie, at least inaccessible.
Then he meets a skunk and the skunk freaks out, now he's in
the tub, he's drying out on a log, he's weeping. At this point
the other ghosts hear his tears, and they pick him up, they fly
him into town, he's weeping, they drop him in the middle of
a dance. It's a Halloween dance! There's a pretty girl dressed
like a ghost, then everyone dies. Then there's a mouse, who is
in love with another mouse. He works all day making shoes
so he can buy a nice dinner for this mouse he is in love with,
but it isn't enough! He has to wash the dishes to pay for the
rest of the meal, and he is so embarrassed, he is weeping and
washing the dishes, because nothing he can do will ever be
enough! When, all of a sudden, the mouse he is in love with
shows up, and washes the dishes right next to him, and kisses

him on the cheek. Then there's a pig dressed as a cop out in his cop car and he gets shot in the face by a bandit! He does not find the bandit, so he goes to get an ice cream. While in line, he gets shot in the face, again! He arrests the whole store! He throws it in a sack and drags it over to prison! Everything goes black.

Everyone who worked on those cartoons is dead now. They've been dead for so long! Their children are dead, and their grandchildren are dead, and even their memories are dead, and they died drunk, and broke, and they put their whole lives into things that will outlive us all. When the dead animators' wives, who are also dead, come home, it just takes their breath away. Someone put a fresh amaryllis in a beautiful vase. It is three feet tall and it keeps growing. It is blooming. The whole room is full of flowers now. In the next room is death. Death wears a white suit and white cowboy boots and a white bolo tie and such a fine white hat and has a horse's skull, perfectly clean, for a face. Death loves it here, because it's so beautiful. The flowers are everywhere. I hope we never have to leave.

OK so it's 1850. The President, having single-handedly murdered thousands of Mexicans to get at their land because he wanted it to be as white as his fucking bones, which you'll see soon, when he dies, I promise, invents California. But the thing about California is that California *had already been invented* as a fictional land populated by black Amazons going as far back as romance novels of the 1500s, and its statehood was precipitated by a revolution of settlers against Mexicans.

What I mean to say is that California is a shining example of the great American art of rebranding. But just you wait till 1901. Why? Because 1901 marks the most important invention of the twentieth century: *vacation*.

Sam says to Eleanor, "I don't know what to make you for breakfast. I'm not good at breakfast. But it's important. And I don't know what I'd do without you. I mean I do. Let's play this out. In one story, right, I'd still be in the woods. And either I'd have become one of those people whose life has really really focused itself to a startling degree, and I'd be utterly and completely aware of every inch of the world around me, I'd be as one with the fucking land or I'd have drowned or I'd have been picked up before the sky split open and drowned our whole summer camp and we fled to the woods for however long it took for us to get rescued by sirens and just gone through my life without you, and maybe I'd love someone else, but they wouldn't be you, so would it count? Probably. But it shouldn't. Because it'd be less good, without you. Who the fuck wants things to be less good? Who among us wishes life had less beauty and wonder in it? The other night a whole apartment got blackbagged and tossed into a van and nobody will ever see anyone in that apartment ever again. The other day a seven-year-old got shot by a cop because the cop thought the kid's hand was a gun and they won't let anyone move the body so the parents have to walk over their kid's dead body every day to go to work, and they're hourly, so. I know that jamming that in there at the end makes it feel poignant, like I'm trying to make a point here. But I just don't know what else to say sometimes. Everything feels like a lot, all the time. And you're here. And I made toast. And the coffee's on. And I love you so very much." He says this before something really important happens, that changes his life forever. Eleanor says, "Oh," she says, "Honey," and she puts her head against him. Outside are the secret police. Did you forget about them? That's because they're secret, and they are professionals, and very good at their job!

Shh!

"Sam, I love you so much. And it's so hard sometimes to tell you how much I love you, not because I love you too much!, but because it seems so hard for you to love yourself! I want to hit you in the fucking face and tell you to snap out of it! Sam! You have a beautiful heart! You have a thick cock! I hate saying that and I am saying it because I want you to feel good about yourself because you make me feel good about myself! You make people feel good about themselves! Dinner is literally the least of what you have to offer, and it is delicious! Sam! Please! I love you! Snap out of it!"

Please!

OK SO IT'S DECEMBER OF 1969. Fred Hampton has just been killed in his bed by the Cook County State's Attorney's Office in conjunction with the Chicago Police Department and the Federal Bureau of Investigation. He has just taught a political education course at a local church. It was unequivocally a political assassination. Hampton was about to forge an understanding between some churches, some local gangs, and the Black Panthers, to help bring purpose to the youth to unite them in defense of their community from the police and the state. He was drugged by someone in his room who was working for the FBI, and in the middle of the night the police broke down his door and assassinated him. His pregnant girlfriend was in bed with him when they broke down the doors and opened fire between ninety and ninety-nine times. The Panthers in the room fired one shot. It was not the first shot fired. After they cleared everyone out they shot his drugged body twice in the head. Again, he was drugged by a man he thought was his friend, who was being paid by the FBI. He united everyone. Everyone listened to him. He helped everyone understand we are all in the same struggle. He helped everyone understand that the police are a force to be used against us while we pay them for the privilege of the violence they visit upon us day in and day out. I'm sorry I said killed earlier. He was murdered. In his bed. And when you're murdered for political purposes, it's an assassination. He was twenty-one years old. He had devoted his life to the uplifting of his community. Not a day goes by that this world isn't poorer for his not being in it. He was, unequivocally, the best of us. And we murdered him, unequivocally, in his sleep. So what does that say about America?

Out the window is a great speckled bird. It's wearing a crown
of thorns. The crown is on fire. The great speckled bird is
looking you right in the eye. It has got absolutely nothing to
say to you. Not one thing. Your whole life is stretched out
before you, and what did you do with it?

This was the winter Sam learned how to make buttermilk
chicken, which is where you clip the tips off the wings of a
chicken and then brine it in two cups of buttermilk and two
tablespoons of kosher salt, and you just let it sit like that, overnight, ideally, then scrape off the buttermilk, don't wash it off
but like use your hands, you're not trying to be thorough, and
roast it at 425 for twenty minutes then 400 for the next forty
minutes or until the juices run clear. If you want to be fancy
you could spatchcock it, sear it in a skillet, then transfer to
the oven. You can cook some green beans in butter and lemon,
and maybe make mashed potatoes, thank God you bought
that thing of buttermilk for the chicken. It was the winter he
decided to get in a fight with Eleanor but she wasn't home, so
Sam couldn't get in a fight with her, even though he wanted to,
and then it turned out that it wasn't so much that Sam wanted
to get in a fight with Eleanor so much as it was that Sam, it
turned out, felt a deep and extreme dissatisfaction with the
way his life was going, despite the apartment they could afford and the love he and Eleanor had built, this glowing life
of theirs, because it was a really good life they had!, but still,
Sam didn't have a career, he barely ever had any money, his
days dragged on and on while he waited for work to come in
and people to pay him for the things he'd done for them, for

three years now he'd done everything he could, applied for every job and grant and begged and pleaded for work that he would get and pray to be paid for, every steady job collapsed with the companies that collapsed under whatever it was that we all needed, which was everything, all the time. It was the winter he really finally wondered how long a life like this could last. That was this winter.

"Sam, tell me that story, the one about the future, where it's winter."

In the future, where it's winter, the sky opens up and snow falls and falls and falls and falls. Eventually the whole world is covered in snow, and they'd either starve or freeze to death in this apartment, which is a relatively decent enough place to die in, Sam felt, though he could tell she maybe didn't feel the same way, and at this point in the narration a piano kicked in, and handclaps, but menacing. Eleanor said, "Then what happens?" In Sam's head he just stared at her, thinking about forever, but out loud he said, "You emerge from the building, shining, and new, naked but for a gigantic fur coat, which turned out to be a way more practical decision than it would have otherwise seemed, having completely forgotten about me. The world stands before you dressed up as an endless and vast promise, and you are the only person who can keep that promise. All is before you, and your glorious gigantic coat, which is more beautiful than anyone could have imagined. Later, but not much later, in the snow, you come across a man, weeping." "Is it you? Are you weeping, baby?" "No, darlin. It's not me." And it's true. It isn't.

Once upon a time, Eleanor took Sam on a vacation. Sam had never been on a real vacation as an adult in that he had never had enough money to pay for the time it took to go somewhere to really get away from it all for a minute. They picked a town and there they went, remaining virtually anonymous, like all tourists. Nobody wants to look at a tourist. They're the worst. So Sam and Eleanor walk around town. They hold hands. They lean into each other. Nobody here knows them. They get in the car they rented and drive to get some groceries. They repair to the cabin they rented, it's a very nice cabin, it's even nicer than their apartment, which costs them $2,250 a month, only to discover that it is, suddenly, cocktail hour. But first, Sam brines the pork chops in apple cider vinegar and brown sugar and hot sauce. Later, he is going to slap them in the skillet. Sam wants a drink. Eleanor makes it for him because Sam's hands are peeling and chopping carrots and dropping them into a pan with butter sitting in olive oil and some maple syrup. Meanwhile, Eleanor puts the rice in the rice cooker, thank God there's a rice cooker here (and after using it they bought one (I guess this will really drive home what I said before about "once upon a time")), with a lot of butter and a splash of white wine vinegar. Sam's reducing balsamic and whisking in some mustard to thicken it into something resembling tar. Outside there's a field in a meadow. It's dusk. You can tell because of the smell, of how dusk smells, like a door opening into an unlit room. Eleanor brought Sam here and he's fixing dinner. He doesn't know where anything is and it's cute. He isn't even getting cranky or panicking because they've been working on that, on Sam learning how to accept the world as it is, which is doomed and wondrous.

Later Eleanor is going to put some mascara on him so that he looks pretty because his lashes are so long, it is fucked up that his lashes are that long, and he does not appreciate them or do enough with them, he could be the leader of the free world with lashes like that, but here they are, leaderless, waiting on dinner, which will never be ready.

They sit at the table they dragged onto the porch and they eat. When they're done, night falls all over the place like the future. We zoom out wide, past Sam and Eleanor. In the distance there's a rumbling of faint-hearted applause, then the clouds burst. Lightning and thunder get shit-faced in celebration. Four wolves jump headlong into the river, and accidentally drown. Some birds attempt to carry off their bodies under the cover of a natural disaster. Imagine a thing like that. The woods hold their breath.

Snap out of it, Sam!
For, somewhere, out in the
vastness of the American
February, spring
training has begun!

OK SO IT'S 2018. The most popular song in America is this song about working yourself to the fucking bone so that one day you will have enough money to buy your entire hometown and employ absolutely everyone there and fire everyone who ever caused you pain in your childhood so that they could never find work again and have their souls crushed completely. It is the most popular song in the history of America. Meanwhile Major League Baseball asks Congress to please pass the Save America's Pastime Act to make sure that baseball should be exempt from having to pay minor league ballplayers a minimum wage, because it would ruin the national pastime if they had to do that! Anyway that's how the federal government saved America's pastime.

Alright say that one day the President announced that there were secret police and the secret police went around blackbagging people and it was terrifying and nobody knew who was a secret police or what you did to get blackbagged and so how do you talk about this with people when talking about this could get you blackbagged and the person you were talking to could be the one blackbagging you or the room, the room could blackbag you, because that happened just last week? A little girl, she was four, asked her dad about the secret police, and her dad told her that they were some mean bad men the President made up to kidnap people so everyone would be too scared to talk about things with each other and maybe one day they'd just get used to it and forget and then what would happen then, he asked her, and she started to think, and as she thought, the walls of their apartment turned out to be full of the secret police. So then what happens?

Sam walked in the door. He was full up with magnificent intentions. Eleanor was out. Sam sat down. Ten minutes later he took out his phone. He checked his bank account. He rent his garments. WOE AND CALAMITY ABOUND IN THE FINANCIAL SECTOR, announced the news. "Tell me about it," said Sam. POOR SPENDING HABITS AND A LACK OF CONSISTENT INCOME CONTRIBUTE TO FISCAL INSECURITY AND A GENERAL SENSE OF INADEQUACY. Sam stared out the window. NATIONWIDE, THERE IS A PALPABLE SENSE OF DISAPPOINTMENT. There was a brief commercial break where the President asked everyone to text a number to send him five dollars to fight the war being raged against him at all times of the day and also the night, even now, at this very moment, in the fallow fields of our youth, and then there was a commercial for burgers, for the way they taste, the cheese holding you and the burger like a blanket, and you can *smell* the burger, you can taste it in the air, it's heavy with promise, the clouds are low and wisping, and winter is nowhere to be found. THE DISAPPOINTMENT IS ALMOST VIOLENT. The news came back, and then paused, just enough for Sam to think he'd caught his breath. CAN YOU FEEL IT? And Sam could, and Sam did, and then the news said, TODAY THE POLICE CONSIDERED DETAINING YOU FOR YOUR INABILITY TO CONTRIBUTE TO SOCIETY BUT COULD NOT QUITE DECIDE HOW TO WRITE IT UP IN THE BOOKS, AND SO YOU WERE LET GO. WERE YOU, goes the news, EVEN AWARE

OF HOW CLOSE YOU CAME TO HAVING A BLACK BAG THROWN OVER YOUR HEAD BEFORE BEING TOSSED IN A VAN WHERE NOBODY WOULD EVER KNOW YOUR NAME AGAIN?

Sam took the news out back and set it on fire. He watched it burn. Sam felt that enough was enough as regards today. Sam knew that civil disobedience could only take you so far. This is what Sam told himself on a regular basis. Sam texted Johnny, *civil disobedience can only take you so far.* Days later, Johnny replied, *Yes but one day it'll be summer.*

But not yet.

ONE DAY THE ANGELS WILL COME, one day the plants will be watered, one day we'll all have enough money and the mighty will be thrown from their thrones and the hungry will be filled with good things and the rich will be sent away empty. One day this will all be different. One day the sun will start staying out longer and longer until one day the sun started staying out for longer and longer. Bit by bit, the mountains of long-accumulated snow were melted into rivers that would, one day, drown us all, given half the chance. Birds started singing. Small children emerged from their hibernation, alive and, I guess, well. The light coming off the buildings felt somehow alive, you could almost hear Prospect Park waking up over the subways and buses and sirens. Thirty-two babies were born the second the snow finally melted for good and then, suddenly, all our hands were clean. There was no official tally for how many people or buildings or buses or cars or plants or books or dinners or food carts or pets or trees or dreams that the secret police had blackbagged, but, on the websites devoted to cataloging reports from the internet, it was estimated to be anywhere between four hundred and two thousand that winter. Then the secret police came for winter. In the end, they'll come for you, too.

When Sam was in middle school and high school, he used to babysit for neighbors for ten or twenty bucks a pop. In college, every summer he worked for minimum wage in a coffee shop selling officially licensed coffee in a chain bookstore, until the summer he worked at an art camp as a counselor and sculpture TA and had one day off a week where he would go with whoever else had that day off to drink rum runners and watch pirates chase after their long-dead youth in dark and cold rooms, and then when he graduated, he got a job as a fishmonger. It was great: he made $10 an hour, forty hours a week, he had health insurance, he got to use the PA system often, he lived with four friends in a five-bedroom house in South Philadelphia and the whole house was $1,350 a month, then he moved to New York and went to grad school, where he took out $50,000 in loans to cover the second year and another $20,000 to live off of, which he would have to pay back at nine percent interest and, luckily for him, at a rate dictated by his income according to his tax returns, provided he was making above the national poverty line, which at that time was $10,830 and is today $12,880.

In New York, Sam had a series of incredible relationships that ended, and he dated several women he should have been nicer to, and once he fell in love with a married woman for a summer, but we don't really have much of a say regarding who we fall in love with, especially when they really want us to fall in love with them, and obviously it didn't work out, and then, finally, years after that summer where the sky opened up and their whole camp drowned and they were together in the woods alone for weeks, he and Eleanor were reunited. At one point, it was no longer, technically, legal to be a poet, and so things got a little weird for Sam as regards to how he could afford to live, and he worked as a nanny, which he loved and which paid pretty well when there were hours to work, and he made maybe $14,000 a year, under the table, working we'll say nine months out of the year, occasionally picking up some copywriting or editing for various websites that needed to have words on them for people to stare at on their phones for maybe five seconds, then all of a sudden and without any warning, the kids ended up getting older, so they didn't need him really, and Sam had little to no work, and then Geronimo (you'll meet him soon!) got him a job doing freelance proof-reading and fact-checking, which was great, so long as there was work, and there wasn't always work, so this was a really weird and inconsistent situation, which is incredibly stressful and usually involves you using your credit card to buy groceries so you can eat, which, let me tell you, is not the best plan in the long term.

Sam and Eleanor met each other again fifteen years after summer camp, five years before today. So now Sam's thirty-three, just like Christ when he died and Roy Halladay when he threw a perfect game and then a postseason no-hitter just five months later, the second no-hitter ever in baseball post-season history, making him the only pitcher in the history of the world to have thrown a perfect game and a no-hitter in the same season. While I've been telling you all this, Eleanor is doing the dishes, and Sam is cleaning the bathroom floor, but not as well as he could, and it's entirely possible Eleanor will say, "Baby, I'm so glad you cleaned this, but can you, next time, try a little harder? Because there's still stuff everywhere, and I know you're trying, but if I just have to go back and do it then we're not doing it together, you know?" And he does know, and he'll do better, I hope, I hope, I hope!

In the morning, Eleanor came and wrapped her arms around
Sam where he sat with his coffee. She said, "I had the strangest dream last night."

She shook her head, which was full of disbelief. In his
heart Sam knew a great storm was brewing. He could feel
thunder rolling in hard under a cloud built like a minivan.
Doom knows your name and has a firm grasp of the particu-
lars. Sam felt electric, he felt ecstatic, he felt primarily alive, it
was great, you should try it. He closed his eyes and breathed
real deep.

He said, with a smile, "Tell me all about it," and she told
him all about it.

It's summer camp. The air's close and everything's wet. Last
night there were hot dogs and the moon got so low it was the
only thing in the sky. Eleanor wakes up in her bunk and the
moon is still sitting like that. She walks outside. She can hear
everyone but can't see anyone. She wanders around the camp.
She jumps in the lake and it's cold and incredible. She takes
an outdoor shower to wash the lake water away with more
lake water. Eleanor is ignoring the moon and the moon is not
indifferent about it. Eleanor is looking for Sam. She is aware
at this point that it's a dream. The moon is never that big, and
the sky is never the same in the day as it is at night. Nothing
about this is right but it also isn't terrible. Eleanor is looking
for Sam. Sam is not in the cabins and he's not in the lake and
he's not in a canoe and he's not in the trees or the woods or
in the offices or on the single bus parked in the dirt lot and

Sam isn't in the dirt, so Eleanor climbs up the tallest tree she can find, the one straight to the moon, to see if Sam is there, because she just remembered something she has to tell him, and she can't wait to tell him, it'll make his whole entire day.

Listen, if you were expecting more from a dream, I don't know what to tell you!

Sam wakes up to an email from his friend Lev. Lev believes firmly in the nonhierarchical path of anarchy, a system that espouses skepticism of all authority and that calls for the abolition of the state, which will never love you. Anarchy is, at its core, a system which endeavors to allow all people to live freely, equally, and safely, with decisions made communally. It's a beautiful thing which exists in utter opposition to the state, which, again!, will never! love! you! Lev also likes grappa; he absolutely loves it. And the Russian baths. Especially in winter. God, have you gone to the baths in winter? Have you felt your skin snap as you leave? It's incredible! So anyway, Lev emails Sam and says, *Hey Sam, do you still need a job, because it is possible that I have one for you here at my firm where I work*, and Sam emails Lev back and says, *oh my god yes wait are there still jobs?* and Lev emails Sam and says *Yes, lol*, and Sam emails back, *yes please can I please apply to be considered to have this job*, and Sam does indeed immediately write a cover letter and tweak his résumé based on the description of the job Lev then gives him.

Out the window, in the distance, is a great speckled bird. In its arms are the dreams of a nation. If you are not careful, it will look you right in the eye. Whatever happens after that is between you and your God. I'm sorry. It just is.

Now Sam has a job! It is a real job with a decent salary and benefits and vacation days, holy fucking shit!, and then, seconds after Sam got the job, Lev got hit by a bus, and died instantly, his limbs strewn down Broadway, a list of names of members of the secret police in his pocket, two secrets on his lips, and love in his heart.

But so now Sam has a job!

HELL YEAH.

TODAY ON HIS LUNCH BREAK Sam called his representative on the phone but they were busy, so Sam reapplied for his income-based repayment plan for his student loans because he now has a stable and easily reported income. In fifteen more years, assuming the world is still around, isn't it weird that we think about this now, about if the world will still be around, whether California will be placed into the sea, like a plot, the coastlines redrawing themselves like certain doom? When New York is under water will the trains still be delayed, and by how long? I was going to talk more about Sam's student loans, what would happen in fifteen years, but it doesn't matter. You have loans. You already know. You know exactly what this is about. Meanwhile, Sam stood in the bathroom at work and looked at himself in the mirror until his whole life changed. Then someone else came into the bathroom, and Sam ate his lunch at his desk like a person with little choice in the matter. Outside, the sun was shining.

It's worth noting, on such a beautiful day as this!, that God isn't in the Constitution, or in any the amendments, outside, abstractly, the right to religious freedom, and it's *absolutely* worth noting that the first time God shows up in America is 1864 when IN GOD WE TRUST got put on the two-cent piece, and then UNDER GOD got added to the pledge of allegiance in 1954, and after that IN GOD WE TRUST got put on all legal tender, and was subsequently made the motto of this nation, replacing the original one of E PLURIBUS UNUM, meaning OUT OF MANY, ONE, we are all one people, one nation, made of all these individuals, with their hearts full of blood and dreams, whose current creed we got from what we stamped on money, which is, at least in America, a whole bunch of paper that we really hope adds up to something.

The plants in the apartment were, for the record, as follows: Muppet Baby, whose leaves were like fingers the color of fresh grass and who was not currently, but would soon be, dying; Franklin Pierce, who was spiky, and dark, and whose wife suffered from depression, and whose children all died in childhood, every one of them, and who opposed the abolitionist movement, and, unlike its namesake, this plant was not, and would possibly never be, dying; Mr. President, a small jade plant who was thriving and stubborn for most of this narrative, right up until the end; Guglielmo Marconi the Inventor of the Radio, a real large plant with leaves like a tree made of vines and who was strung with lights and stayed low to the ground by the two low-slung yellow chairs in the living room; several unnamed supporting actors of various sizes and dimensions, all of them in relatively small pots, some with tall stalks reaching to the sky, others low and cranky and threatening death, plotting their cruelties by kitchen windows; Evidence of Alien Life, who started as what looked like an angry pinecone, then one day three tendrils emerged, and the tendrils, overnight or over time, unfurled into hard bright blossoms, and then they kept growing, curling ever upward towards the ceiling, where they made their way to the window, their motives and origins unknown to this very day; The First Lady, who was beautiful, and died that way too; Big Boy, a truly enormous elephant ear plant whose roots threatened the confines of her brass bucket; Warren Beatty, a moonshine snake; The Rite of Spring, a bird's nest fern Sam has absolutely managed to help thrive by watering lightly around the edges and misting periodically; General Gorgeous, a burgundy-and-gold croton who cannot decide if they want to live or die; The Economy, a thriving and a-bit-too-on-the-nose-named money plant; Nope, an enormous yellow-and-green snake plant kept on the floor of the bedroom, at least four feet tall and thriving; a peperomia ginny named Opening Day, full of hope and promise; and three hanging plants named the Ghosts of Christmas Past, Present, and Future; and, of course, the rubber tree plant, last seen slowly divesting itself of its worldly possessions, now no longer even discretely waiting for the end to come, but racing towards it, headfirst, like oblivion was a destination you arrive at on your own.

One day, not today, but soon, real soon, each and every one of those plants are going to need to be watered. And nobody will be able to help them. Even though their very lives depend upon it. So just think about that.

Is it worth talking about how the various depictions of revolution and rebellion from the '60s all seem silly today? That we've turned the language corny, we've turned love into a commodity, free love into a sad weird joke, we've made the Panthers into anything but what they were, it doesn't help that the yippies became capitalists but maybe that's what happens with white revolutionaries when they don't win is they sell out.

Anyway maybe there isn't really a point here, but I think it's worth thinking about the fact that we no longer take revolution seriously, and I think it's worth asking why it is that our depictions of revolutions are just a series of jokes intended to make us all feel better about how things turned out while we wait and see if it's time yet to water the plants.

OK it's today, and it's time to water the plants. Every single one of them, except the ones that don't need it, and only as much as they need, because otherwise they'll drown, and they'll die, and it'll be all your fault, but so long as you don't do that, they'll thrive, and they'll be beautiful, and your home will be full of life, of love. So long as you don't let them die. Meanwhile, Eleanor put her tits in Sam's mouth. She put her hands around his neck. She closed her eyes until she was in a small room, much like this one, just smaller, and filling, gradually, with light. As the light grew to fill the entirety of the room and then her heart, her body, the whole entire fucking world, she pulled Sam away and looked him in the eyes. "I love you" is what the script had said she'd said to him, just then, but we couldn't hear. The curtains dropped. The audience rose from their seats, and filed out, into the mystery of the rest of their lives.

"How was work?" asked Eleanor, walking in the door to Sam taking chicken breasts marinated in barbecue sauce out of the fridge, firing up the grill pan, starting the rice in the rice cooker, getting some butter and olive oil and salt and pepper and dried basil for the frozen corn he was going to cook, and Sam said, "Well I made the coffee and scheduled the lunch for next week's office meeting, we're gonna have Korean tacos, and then I moved things around in documents so that it looked professional, and I spent three hours renaming and migrating files, for efficiency, in the future." Eleanor dropped her bag and kicked off her shoes and flung herself onto the couch. "Sam," she said, "today I did work on a screen. My boss told me something important about her eggs, she keeps them in the fridge, next to a carton of eggs, it's a joke, she says, but also it isn't, she doesn't wink she just bares her teeth but it's the same thing." Sam pours her a glass of very cold white wine. He brings it to her as she kicks off her shoes in the seat for this purpose. "Sam," she says, taking the glass, and sighing, her bag dropped on the floor, where Sam picks it up to put it on a hook, "What if we just said the weird parts of our days." "Oh thank god. Nobody, you know, needs to relive a job." Eleanor smiled, looked him in the eye, said, "I love only you, Sam," and Sam said, "Death to our common enemies," and they clinked their glasses. He went back to the stove and turned the chicken. The sun hadn't even set yet. Eleanor put a record on.

Sam's coworkers still didn't know what, exactly, Sam did, as, again, Lev died after hiring Sam but before Sam started, and also Lev seems to have believed in communicating through handwritten memos, which were, eventually, scanned and filed, which was probably going to be part of Sam's job, but now we'll never know. So Sam just sort of did whatever peo-

ple needed done, and they paid him $50,000 a year, which
was substantially more than he'd made before, and considering, again, that no one knew what he did there, this bring us
to today. Today, there's a weird sound out the window. A low,
echoing thrum, with a sort of tinny whine in the background.
No one can tell where it's coming from. Usually there's con-
struction, nonstop, but this is a different sort of sound. Sam
goes to the window. The workers are out there. But there's
just this sound. Sam looks at the street. He looks across to the
windows of the buildings, but all he sees is the sun reflected
back at him over and over again. Sam looks up at the sky.
His coworkers ask him about the next happy hour. Sam tells
them he will prepare for them a cocktail. Everyone becomes
excited. No one has ever made them a cocktail before in their
lives. Sam goes to the store and gets some gallon pitchers with
the petty cash. He will batch out some cocktails in them. Not
now, but eventually, he will realize he absolutely needs to water them down. At a holiday party, in the future, one of the
firm's principals will leave early, and Sam will say, "You never
stay and drink with us," and Eleanor will miss this interac-
tion, and the principal will turn to Sam, and start a drinking contest, eventually Sam will sneak off to the bathroom to
boot and rally, but the principal will follow him in, too late!,
and ask if he is in there throwing up, "You're not throwing
up in there, are you, Sam? You're not a quitter?" which Sam
will not hear as a plea until much much later, and Sam will
say, "No way I would never do something like that," and they
will go back out there, and Sam's coworkers, seeing his face,
through the night, will take his drink out of his hand as soon

as the principal puts it in there, they will save his liver, in the car home he will hang his head out the window, Eleanor'll sigh, she'll hold his hand, she'll hope he won't throw up, and he won't!, she will march him into the bathroom to just disinfect his whole mouth a few times, and they will crawl into bed, and Sam'll muttering apologies, all night, "I apologize," I forgive you, Sam, "I apologize," It's OK, Sam, "I apologize," until they're both, finally, asleep in each other's arms. Anyway that's the future. Back to today!

At the end of the day today, Sam goes home. He gets on a nearly empty train. It screeches along the tracks. This is comforting, Sam thinks, then he gets off the train, into the grocery store, gets a rotisserie chicken, a baguette, haricot vert (they're skinnier, it's great, trust me!), some lemons, leaves the store, walks through door, puts the chicken in the oven to stay warm, and starts making the rest of dinner. Eleanor comes in and kisses him right on the mouth. She is so happy to see him. Sam's heart is in his chest. It has donned its fiery crown. Its wings fill his body. Light pours from his mouth. Dinner is ready. Sam fucks Eleanor with a desperate tenderness the world has never before seen. He holds her close all night, his eyes at a point just past her head, watching the loose strands of her hair move with his breath. Eleanor is dreaming of the moon rising up out their window. The moon asks her how things are going. Eleanor tells the moon that everything is incredible. The moon tells her she's pregnant. The moon tells her it isn't like she imagined. Eleanor tells the moon that this is a dream, she has no idea what she has imagined, because she is asleep! In the corner of his eye, Sam nearly sees the angels. Eleanor, in her sleep, tells the moon exactly what to do with its fucking imagination. Sam kisses Eleanor on the cheek. He drinks some water. Eventually, he falls asleep.

Somewhere in a castle is a German orchestra. They've been stuck there for a month. The castle's in Italy, surrounded by a vast and endless forest. The forest is full of wolves. They're stacked three or four high. They prowl. The orchestra is tuning up. They've been at it for a month. The wolves are waiting. Sam's asleep. Eleanor's asleep. The moon's up in space, where it lives, circling the Earth, conducting the tides, and watching us sleep, like a creep. The moon hates cops, the moon hates debt, that either are necessary, this is why there are floods, why the water will, one day, wash us away. To ascribe anything else to the moon would be ridiculous. It would be just completely ridiculous. The moon knows your secrets. It knows every one of them. It's in the sky and it's in your dreams and the secret police can't ever touch it.

Now it's summer.
Thank God.

THE STREETS OF BROOKLYN are lined with mountains of trash just boiling alive in the sun, which is eternal, and unrelenting, from six in the morning to eight thirty at night. Forty-five babies have just come into the world, screaming. Like right now, as I'm telling you this. Imagine that! From Sam and Eleanor's apartment building's roof, which you cannot get to, you can see the arch across the street from Prospect Park. One winter, the Eagles won the Super Bowl. But now it's summer. Since 1901, stone eagles have sat on pylons atop the park's entrance, where they eye you, warily. Meanwhile Johnny moved to Berlin and took up boxing, which is why we haven't heard from him in a bit and may never hear from him again, but he is, mostly, very happy. He lives in a bunker. He loves the way the sky looks during a storm there. He could not begin to describe it. It is sometimes just so nice to find creation more than you can bear. Today Sam's second favorite tennis player has advanced to the finals of an obscure and hitherto unknown tournament while Sam's second favorite tennis player's own personal mother, a former Malaysian princess who renounced her title and claim to the throne to pursue a computer science degree and marry a Greek house painter, burns an effigy of the Cuyahoga River. The eagles are restless. The boathouse in the park is beautiful this time of year. I really wish you could see it. When Eleanor walked in the door, Sam announced, "The boathouse was so beautiful today. I really wish you could have seen it." Immediately Eleanor's phone rang. Earlier today (it's the weekend), Sam cooked some chicken in white wine vinegar and black pepper, and he cut up and sautéed green beans in some browned butter, and mixed that all up with some pasta and pesto, and stuck it in the fridge. He takes it out to get it to room temperature, and then adds some little bits of mozzarella, the perlini ones, and gets out a white wine and all the ice in the world. Eleanor comes out of the bathroom, where she went to take the call. She looks like she has seen a ghost, in that she looks startled by mortality in a way that feels a little inevitable, but also incredibly thrilling. Later, Eleanor will tell him that the tests are fine. It wasn't a bad abnormality. It was just an abnormal abnormality. Nothing's changed. The world keeps turning. In thirty years the coasts'll be impossible. After that they retired to the country. Sam died younger than anyone really expected, due mostly to his wild heart. Off in the distance was a hawk in flight.

The President's on a boat with a knife in his teeth. Except this isn't the President, and everyone is drowning. Then the river freezes over. In the distance is a castle. Your whole life is a ghost story told 'round a campfire you could never even imagine, so stop it. Please.

Oh, I'm sorry, did you miss spring? Are you wondering what happened there? So did everyone! Sam's birthday is the first day of spring and it fucking snowed six inches! The snow didn't melt until May 1! By Memorial Day it's gonna be ninety degrees! I don't know what to tell you here!

I keep forgetting you might not know about Prospect Park. Prospect Park is 526 acres in size, whatever that means, and was designed by Frederick Law Olmsted and Calvert Vaux, who also designed Central Park, which is 843 acres. Widely known for its intricate manmade wetlands where a woman once let Sam finger her at night under the moon drinking old-fashioneds from flasks, and its glorious trees which some say constitute the bulk of Brooklyn's remaining indigenous forests, a zoo, the first urban-area Audubon center in the nation, an ice rink, the Vale of Cashmere, which is this secluded patch of wilderness that the Mayor of Brooklyn's wife once named after a poem by some sad dead Englishman and that's absolutely all it's ever been known for, a band shell, a carousel, the boathouse, wi-fi hotspots, and, among other things, bike paths. And, oh my God, the Long Meadow. The Long Meadow stretches down the western side of the park, and its ass end contains seven baseball fields. Its pastoral quality is preserved by sheep, who graze at length upon the meadow, now in secret, at night, under cover of darkness. So when the park's dark, that's why, unless it's the secret police. There is not a single time of the year when Prospect Park is not beautiful, but the boathouse at sunset is truly something.

The best thing we can say about the summer is that now that Sam and Eleanor are both fully employed and the sun doesn't set till nearly 8:00 p.m. it is really easy to light the candles and say the prayer as the sun sets. It is really nice to not have to scramble to leave a light going as the others go out.

Sam's wide awake. It's morning. The less valuable aspects of
Sam's job mean that he needs to be at his job before Eleanor
needs to be at hers so that there will be coffee ready for the
employees who matter and who have clear job descriptions
which absolutely anyone could understand. Sam makes Eleanor some coffee and puts it in the fridge. When she gets up
it'll be cold, which is exactly how she likes it. Eleanor takes
an express train eight stops into the city. Sam takes a local
twelve stops. The math here, like all math, is bad. Eventually Sam will get a raise, and, after that, he'll get one every
year. He'll be a valued employee. People just appreciate having
him around in ways they have a hard time expressing, and so
they decide to give him money, to try to express this. Nobody
ever really told them what to do with their feelings, but this
seems right. Sam is startled at four when a truck drives by.
The street out the windows had been closed since before Sam
started. They had to replace the fiber optics and then it turned
out the pipes were rotting so after they dug up the pipes they
had to wait for the people who do the pipes to come and bring
new pipes for the new cables and then they had to pave over
the street again, and after that ConEd had to come and do
the power, and dig up the street, and pave it back up, and it
keeps going like that, each contractor coming once the last
one's finished, forever. The truck was on the sidewalk. Nobody got hurt, it's fine. It was startling, though. Sam fills out
his timesheet with aplomb. Who knows where the hours go?
Whoever the fuck reads these time sheets, that's who. That's it
for the workday. See you tomorrow.

As you probably remember, earlier, Sam was barely employed and pretty depressed, and Eleanor, wanting to do something nice for him, since she couldn't get him a job or erase his student loans or his credit card debt, got Sam a video game wherein he could be there, finally, when the angels come. It was the nicest thing she could do for him at the time. As you probably remember, Sam has a job now. Sam realizes, walking from the train to the office, one morning, that he could go and buy a good coffee grinder and some good coffee and a cold brew device for Eleanor. He could make sure she always had cold coffee in the morning, the way she likes it. It would cost him under $100 to do something that would always, always be nice for her. Money is a stupid, terrible, bullshit thing. But when we have it we can use it to do incredibly nice things for the people we love.

Oh! Remember that castle in Italy full up with a German orchestra, surrounded by a forest, stacked to the brim with wolves, their mouths riddled with menace?

I just wanted to make sure you remembered that it happened.

The castle is still surrounded, by the way, and meanwhile Eleanor's in for her annual thyroid biopsy. Sam's in the waiting room, waiting. They're both in the waiting room, waiting, if we're being honest. If it's gotten cancerous, that's bad, and if the growth has grown to such a size that it impedes her breathing or swallowing or eating then it is going to need to be cut out and there is then a fifty-fifty chance that (briefly: the thyroid is a two-lobed gland beneath your Adam's apple, it secretes three hormones that influence your metabolism, and, in children, these hormones influence growth and development) the other half of her thyroid, the one without the giant nodule growing on it, will pick up the slack and supply her all the hormones she needs, *or* she'll be on thyroid medication for the rest of her life, which means she or Sam will always need to be working until they can afford to retire, it's hard to really see how that's possible, even on Eleanor's salary, because rent and groceries and insurance rates go up faster and at a more competitive rate than her salary could ever, and clearly she'd know if she had trouble swallowing, but how do you now think about this when you're going in to get a giant needle shoved into your neck to sample the tissue of the growth to determine its degree of malignancy, which is absolutely a phrase to turn over and over in your head forever like a raccoon washing a sugar cube in a fucking stream, and she reaches over for Sam's hand and her eyes tear up a little, and Sam looks over at her, and he leans in and kisses her on the head, and he says, "Hey."

God it's so fucking hot. People absolutely love summer but it's so fucking hot. You gotta assume it's because, as a child, the summer is when you felt the most free. I'm not saying that loving summer is related to trauma, I'm just saying there are things we never know how to shake.

She had to swallow during the biopsy, it was a dry swallow, like a reflex, and it's hard to swallow with a large needle jabbed in the base of your neck to sample a tissue in order to confirm that there remains a 10 to 15 percent chance the cells'll one day maybe turn cancerous, and she knows her thyroid's gonna swell way the fuck up, and that she should go home and use ice to bring down the swelling and later a warm compress to break up the clotted blood, but she knows, as soon as she swallows and feels her throat constrict against the, again!, gigantic fucking needle jabbed into the base of her neck to sample a tissue in order to confirm that there remains a 10 to 15 percent chance her cells'll one day maybe turn cancerous, she is going to get up and get out of that room, where she is currently lying on an exam table with her head propped up by a cushion shaped like a triangle to angle her neck where the doctor needs it to be, and she is going to touch Sam on the arm and he'll get up to make her follow-up appointment for her while she walks out the building and across the street and she'll keep walking for one block and cross the intersection and hook a left and say, "Two, please," and Sam'll be right there and they'll get burgers and mimosas. The room's dim and there's a light in her eyes. Her neck's still warm from the sonogram earlier to make sure they knew where precisely to stab the gigantic fucking needle into her neck in the name of medicine, and science. Everyone at the doctor's is polite and sometimes their hands are cold and anyway, if she got cancer and died, she wouldn't have to worry about her student loans anymore, or the credit card debt she accumulated rapidly in college that she has not even told Sam about yet, but that she has done a pretty solid job of mostly paying off. It wouldn't be terrible. She could get high on medical weed and fuck Sam and just love him and die. She and Sam couldn't become domestic partners and he couldn't wear a suit in city hall with her while her palms sweated more than they should because bureaucracy shouldn't be this romantic and then they couldn't meet their friends for drinks later while everyone smiled at their love, which is a beacon, and a light, while cop cars screamed past to drown out a family reportedly living their lives in defiance of the state, and the cop cars would stop right there, because of their love, recognized even by city hall, that gateway to our own personal America, and the cops would get out of the cars, and they'd go home to their loved ones, and they'd break down, and they'd weep.

I'm just kidding, cops don't have hearts or loved ones, because cops can't love. That's why they became cops. If you have the capacity for love, would you become a cop? Would you beat the shit out of people who didn't have homes, would you fail to prevent murders and rapes, would you shoot unarmed children and mothers and fathers and brothers and sisters? Would you do all that? If you had love in your heart would you go out and put people in a six-by-eight-foot cell for the rest of their lives? Would you take away their humanity? That's the job of the police. It isn't to protect you. When a cop shoots an unarmed civilian, who shoots that cop? Who stops that cop? Where is the justice for the dead? Does anyone know? Please?

All around them people were eating food and having a time and three couples in the room were thinking about breaking up. "They'd just break down and weep, Sam," said Eleanor to Sam. I forgot what they were talking about. I'm sorry. I'm doing my best to tell you this, I really am! It's a lot to keep track of! Anyway, Sam looked her right in the eye. "There are no two ways about it." There aren't. He isn't wrong. One couple is breaking up, right now. With each other. At the same time. It's kind of amazing, and the waitstaff has gathered, surreptitiously, to watch. Outside the window is the sky. It is not, at the moment, falling. Sam looks at Eleanor, and Eleanor looks at Sam.

One day there'll come a sunset so beautiful we all just die, and after that is when things really start to get kind of interesting.

After that, the President outlaws food stamps and Medicare and Medicaid. Being poor and being old is undignified. It's un-American. It is, quite frankly, unconstitutional. In response, ten states legalize marijuana, and put the highly taxed proceeds towards public education, statewide pre-K, single-payer health care, and fixing the Goddamn MTA. I'm just kidding, nobody does that. Italy's confused, France is run by Nazis, meanwhile Germany has gone full Baader-Meinhof, and now everyone has to look up what that means. The internet is still touted as the Wild West, in that it remains unincorporated by the state, who could seize its titles at any moment. Christ's disciples hate the poor and love the banks, who now have voting rights, and genders. All of the banks are men now. You're welcome. The angels up in Heaven were still packed in the bedroom with the door closed, flaming swords at the ready, wings singed, hearts full of nothing but light. Downstairs in their apartment are Sam and Eleanor. They don't know what to do. They get a little high and order a pizza. They consume cheese in a reckless fashion. It solves nothing. But they did have pizza. So, I guess, at least, there's that.

Sam went out for a drink with Geronimo, who has just returned from Italy. He had been there so long that honestly I'd completely forgotten about him! But he's one of Sam's best friends, and he's back! Thank God! I can't believe I didn't tell you about him earlier, aside from that stuff about the pipes freezing. Sam has known Geronimo for twelve years. In high school, Geronimo was a volunteer firefighter, and after he graduated undergrad he was an elementary school gym teacher, he had patent leather high-top boat shoes that he told the rudest children were made, the high-top boat shoes, from unicorn skin, and at this news even the rudest children wept, and after that he ghostwrote a drinks blogs for the early internet, and after that he moved to New York, went to grad school, met Sam, very nearly ran an incredibly small museum in Texas, and is currently working his way up the ranks of a university writing center, saving the academic careers of kids whose parents have more money than any of us ever will. Was Geronimo ever married? That's a great question! Geronimo is, in some small ways, a mystery, as all volunteer firefighters must be. Is Geronimo in love with a ghost? Who can say! He is tall, I'll tell you that much. Anyway. Sorry. Geronimo's talking now: "A fucking castle," he said. "Just me, a terrified German orchestra, and the caretaker," and obviously he fell in love with her, and spent his nights awaiting her footsteps at the door, she going barefoot to not startle the orchestra, who were terrified, of the wolves, the moon peering in through the window, the rental car in the driveway, the driveway below the castle, Geronimo pulling up to the castle the first night, the caretaker coming down the path, smiling, a quarto of house red in her hands, a smile on her lips, this followed immediately by the throwing open of the rental car doors and the turning on of the headlights, which is when they started dancing, the whole castle, all night. The wolves were not yet at the doors, the trees appeared utterly lacking in menace, the moon was big as hell. "I was married once," she told the whole castle, and they couldn't help but believe her, "to a ghost, who remains here, with me." Then she smiled like she was fucking with them, and they danced, and the rental car's battery died, and she closed the doors and everyone went into the castle, the German Orchestra to their individual rooms and Geronimo to the kitchen, where a meal of olives and cheese and fresh-baked bread was waiting, they downed another liter of house red, and Geronimo followed the absolutely beautiful caretaker up to his room, for he had prepaid online, and would otherwise not know how to get to it. Later, when she came and knocked on the door, Geronimo would feel a great weight lifting from him, whose presence he was not even aware of before. The flames would play across her face and he could swear he could see his future in them, and then the wind took the candles and the caretaker took him and the moon was nowhere to be found.

The caretaker's name was Isabella. She had long black hair that moved like a river of its own accord and was exactly as long as it needed to be. Geronimo traipses the stairs behind her. The candelabra lights the way. Everything is incredibly romantic. Everyone is freaking out about it. The castle's stones smell wet with the promise of rain. The room's stone, the windows are that diamond-crossed wrought iron with that old glass, you know the kind, thick and warped with bubbles, the sort of thing that reminds you you're looking out through a liquid at a world you pray becomes less solid by the second.

Except it doesn't. At the bar, Geronimo asked Sam what Sam'd been getting up to. "I got a new job and I got a new joke," said Sam. "Oh?" asked Geronimo. "Yeah," said Sam. Sam said, "You know what I like about new moons?" and Geronimo went, "What do you like about new moons, Sam?" And Sam went, "I keep getting older," he went, "and moving inexorably towards my death." Everyone agreed it was a pretty good joke. Years earlier, Isabella was walking along the river. Earlier her high school boyfriend fingered her as she drove down the coast with the top down. As she came she slammed on the brakes to avoid one of those famous leaping deer they have there, and her high school boyfriend was thrown from the car, and impaled upon the antlers of some other, different deer. Isabella got out of the car and walked past the river. She came to a castle. *What in the dear sweet fuck is this doing here*, is what she thought to herself, in Italian. She walked around it five times. The door opened.

"Wait wasn't there something about a nuclear missile, bound for our home of New York City?" "Yeah but we don't talk about it." "Huh." "It seemed like the sort of thing you might approve of, though, I mean the end times." "I mean, I can't fault it. I really can't." "It's a weird world, buddy." "Thank God, Sam." "Thank God, buddy. I missed you so much." "I missed you too, pal!" And then they hug!

Sam sank into bed around three. Eleanor was asleep, having gone out to dinner alone, which she missed so much, eating alone, like she did for years and years before she met Sam, again, and she loves eating with Sam, but sometimes, anyway, earlier Eleanor called her mom, who told her a story about once having sex with a ghost, although she doesn't say *sex* and she doesn't say *ghost*, and Eleanor feels like they're closer in this moment than they have been since the womb, so anyway now Eleanor, asleep, asked her man Sam if he told the moon joke. "I told the moon joke," went Sam. "Thank God," went Eleanor.

Isabella descends the staircase. Geronimo's in the kitchen. He's made an omelet out of goose eggs, duck fat, mozzarella, basil leaves, thinly sliced and overly ripe cherry tomatoes. There's a plate for her, and coffee. He's got three cigarettes going. He's reading the morning paper, although it's in Italian, which he cannot understand. He's a ghost. He's her husband. She takes him in her mouth except it's not her husband and it's not a ghost and the baskets need filling, with fruit, because what else would you do with them? If the basket was empty a ghost would move in. Or a bird. Which is a just a ghost with wings who can leave. None of this is doing her any good. Isabella eats her omelet. A song comes on the radio about watching

the moon. The moon's out the window, in broad daylight, act-
ing a fool. Isabella takes Geronimo in her mouth. He isn't her
husband. Her husband's dead.

The door to the castle opens. A radio sings a song about a
moon. In the kitchen there was a man. He had three cigarettes
going at once. She comes in. She sits down, emphatically, in
the chair across from him on the long low wooden table, and
pours herself a glass of wine. It's a violent pour. It spills over
the sides, onto the table. She doesn't say anything. She downs
the wine. He reaches over and pours, twisting the neck as he
finishes like you always think you see waiters do in films. He
doesn't say anything. She stops. She downs the next glass. She
waits to see if he'll pour another, but nothing happens. She
gets up, and leaves the room.

In the morning, Eleanor describes to Sam the following dream,
more or less: A great speckled bird arrives upon a clearing
in the woods, where the President's bleeding body has been
dragged, through the snow, by some deer. Their antlers take
on a new alphabet. They prop up the President's limbs and
they move him around like a new kind of god. His sad black-
ened blood pools at their feet. It swallows the sun for the rest
of their lives.

Sam texts Geronimo all the things they didn't get to talk
about. It's hard because when you haven't seen a friend in a
while and that friend has a story to tell about falling in love
with a ghost in a castle in Italy while wolves hold an orchestra

hostage there isn't really a lot you can say because you can't compete with a story like that, so you just listen, and later, you can just dump all the information on them. Everyone really appreciates this. *ok so johnny and jane broke up and johnny is in berlin and jane is currently in cleveland. i dont have any answers for that one. have a job! holy shit! know i said it before but it's wild to be able to afford things regularly so on that note next round is absolutely on me and there's this new bar i wanna go to i'll text you the menu*, and Geronimo says, *Yes.* but what is he saying yes to? It could be anything and it could be everything. *do you know about the secret police?* asks Sam in a text but then his message disappeared.

Eventually, Geronimo will have to do something about the woman he's in love with who lives with her husband's ghost in a castle full of a German orchestra who will not leave, because of the wolves, who line the trees like they were other trees, but they're not, they're wolves, and their mouths are a promise that'll rip through your neck until, finally, the light of truth shines down upon your open face.

Eventually, someone is going to have to do something about the wolves.

Geronimo can't stop thinking about Isabella.

In Italy, Isabella comes back into the room. She's changed into one of those loose dresses, a shift dress, the kind where the fabric hugs what it touches when it touches it, where it shifts with the wind, the breeze, the intentions of the room or the wearer, it's the color of white grapes, it looks hand-dyed, there's a sort of cut-away pattern a bit above the bottom. She descends the stairs like that, she ascends the stairs like that, she moves through the room like that and sits down like that, across from him like that, and before she can sit she tells him, "I was in the middle of being finger fucked by my married high school boyfriend when a leaping deer leapt into the road and startled me so I swerved and braked and the boyfriend was thrown from the car and spun through the air which impaled him on the antlers of a completely different deer," Geronimo has taken his glasses off and placed them on the table, she is staring directly at a point just above and to the left of his head, with a great and sincere intensity. She takes a deep breath, she tells him "And so I got out of the car, and I followed the river to the road by the river. I walked through a town and the town was having a party, there was a band on the stage, everyone in the town was sixteen years old, they were dancing, someone gave me a plate of food, I kept walking until the river fell right off the map into the sea, right over there," she looks out the window to show him what she means as though he didn't know what he means and he didn't, not until now, he's staring right at her, she says, "And then the door opened, and I came right in, and I told you this story," she's looking him right in the eyes right now.

"So now what?"

OK SO IT'S 1941. The President wants America to get involved in World War II but America absolutely does not want to get involved in World War II, mostly because America thinks it's totally fine for all those Jews to die, because America's gotta come First, but then, surprise!, the Japanese surprise America by bombing Pearl Harbor in Hawaii, and then America *has* to be involved in World War II. Then in 1963 the President was shot one single time through the back, lung, neck, and throat, by a disgruntled former Marine who was later shot dead by a member of the mob, which could be, loosely, defined as an organized group of criminals who were involved with ensuring the President's 0.2 percent margin win in Illinois (and Chicago in particular) who were then prosecuted, aggressively, by the President's brother, the Attorney General, soon after the President assumed office, in 1961, and then!, after the President was shot, the new President invented, among other things, Medicare, Medicaid, the NEA, the NEH, the Corporation for Public Broadcasting, and free breakfast and lunch for low-income public school students, as part of a large-scale war on poverty and racial injustice. Soon after, the President engaged in a long and vicious military action in Vietnam that left the country utterly divided, and the veterans of this war completely abandoned to homelessness, addiction, and persecution by the police. Once upon a time the President, back when he was the director of the CIA, helped install a truly horrible dictator in Iraq in order to get Iraq to come to our birthday party or something, with Saddam Hussein being on the CIA payroll as early as 1959, and America supporting Iraq's war with Iran by supplying Iraq with guns, money, intelligence, and weapons both biological and chemical. Later, this deal would work out poorly, and America would find itself at war with the man they made ruler so that things would be easier for them, and, later still, that President's son would become President and would want very badly to go kill this man his dad installed as dictator who later became his dad's enemy. He wanted, we could maybe say, if we were feeling generous to a fucking warmonger who created a department to spy on and kidnap Americans in the name of the homeland and its inviolable security, to avenge his dad's mistake. And anyway he totally did go to war with Iraq after terrorists from Afghanistan (who had, previously, been armed and trained by the United States in order to fight off the spread of Russian Communism in the region) killed 2,977 people in multiple attacks on American soil on September 11, 2001. Why did terrorists from Afghanistan inspire a war in Iraq? I couldn't say! But what I *can* say is, at one point in human history, and when and where and by whom is highly and hotly debated, pizza was invented. It is widely available and varies wildly in cost and quality and has brought only joy and happiness to all people. Outside, the wind blows the trees sideways. The leaves flutter and sound like rain.

All around us it's summer. In western North Carolina, a dust storm whips up for a week from the Sahara Desert. Nobody can breathe or go to the batting cages. New York vows to provide no sanctuary, and promises this foreign invader will not enter its sacred borders. Sam goes to the batting cages on Fridays because Sam has Summer Fridays. Sam is remembering to drop his back shoulder a little so he swings up rather than down, he is remembering to close up his stance as he plants his front foot before swinging so he can move his whole body against that giant fucking ball hurtling inexorably homewards. Eleanor is at her desk, looking at houses that they could afford in western North Carolina, I mean like three bedroom houses whose mortgages would be less than their rent, and Sam realizes he should also drop his right hip, his whole right side, he should do this as he breaks from his stance and steps forward to close himself up so he can remember to swing from his hips, this way, thinks Sam, he'll always be getting just under the ball, he won't keep on hitting the ball into the fucking ground all the time, worms have never wronged him, not like birds, thank you to Randy Johnson for showing them what it means to be scared of something. He stands in the corner of the office and practices dropping his hip and shoulder as he swings his hips, he realizes why so many hitters go down on one knee, that it's for leverage, that the body is a lever. The sky right now is really something. Can you see it? The dust is swirling. The winds are all around us. The air is thick with them.

Sam's dad sent Sam this novel about the end of baseball because Sam's dad loves Sam and Sam loves baseball. In the book, there was, all of a sudden!, a sudden outbreak of a disease wherein, if so many human bodies gathered together in any sort of proximity to watch a sporting event, your blood would immediately set itself on fire inside of your body until the fire was outside of your body, and then, after that, you died. Major League Baseball, high as fuck off their legal wins declaring all ballplayers to be seasonal workers, like lifeguards, and therefore not eligible for pensions or health insurance, decided that baseball should keep happening, despite this disease which only happened when so many human bodies gathered to watch a sporting event, because if people couldn't come to ballgames they'd make less money. America agreed the ballplayers were all greedy and bad, because if you wanted to be paid fairly for your labor and have health insurance you were basically a criminal begging for handouts, and America hates criminals, and handouts, which is why America invented prisons and wins every year at the annual How Many Prisoners Do You Have contest. That year the Rule 4 draft was five rounds, and, throughout America, college seniors watched and waited with their families and friends, as their names were never called, and their dreams died right there, on television, for all the nation to see. Soon after this nobody really wanted to play baseball again for little money and no job security, it just lost its appeal.

Overall, the book was widely derided for its relatively ridiculous premise, but it was much better than that shitty bildungsroman about the glove-first shortstop's dalliance with the yips. When baseball actually ended, it was because there was a total labor collapse. Baseball had worked so long and so hard at finding ways to not pay its players while coming up with new rules to increase the time it could air commercials and maximize profits. What this led to was young players ultimately deciding that, since baseball would not pay them, they would play other sports, and finally there was no more available talent, and baseball died, alone, with nobody watching, the lights still on, and all available airtime sold.

OK that's not exactly how it went, but it was the prettiest way to say it. What happened was that Major League Baseball got Congress to institute an actual draft, and they began drafting Americans to force them to play baseball, but this worked out very badly, and people got mad, and then they stormed the statehouse, so, while Congress allowed Major League Baseball to claim all players the teams drafted belonged to the teams entirely, the players union being essentially the same as any other union that wasn't for the police, in that they were there to secure labor for ownership (I'm sorry I know that's deeply unfair there are lots of really good unions but the only ones with any real power belong to the cops and if you have any questions about that I would ask you in what other profession could you be almost guaranteed to keep you job and pension after gunning people down in the fucking streets, also the player's union is a fucking joke, just look at how they sold away the rights of minor leaguers for fucking nothing), it was all a very bad scene, and eventually there were only ten players left alive, but the problem was that the TV rights had already been sold in massive deals, and still had to be honored, so, eventually, baseball games were just shots of empty stadiums, punctuated lengthily by commercials. It was, in its own way, incredibly beautiful.

Sam watched the last ballgame. It happened in the future. The listless announcers, hired for their capacity to convincingly read sponsored content, attempt to describe absolutely nothing. Sam cannot look away. This is the death of something he has loved, his whole life, live, on air. It is the slowest thing he has ever seen. "What are you doing, baby?" asked Eleanor. "Watching part of America die live on TV."

Meanwhile, in Florida, people cannot go into their pools, because of the snakes. Also, off the coast is a hurricane, and on the ground is a tornado. Very small lizards climb to the tops of the screened-in porches. In Florida, everyone has built wonderful closets, to hide in. An alligator watches through its one good eye. Let's back up a bit, though. Let's take it all in. Florida! O, Florida! What more can I say about Florida? Well, I can say that Florida was invented by the conqueror Juan Ponce de León, who invaded its land and raped its peoples. To say he invented it is, when it comes down to it, sinful and shameful. Your invention cannot be credited to your killer. I'm sorry that I keep fucking this up, but I do feel that it's important or at least maybe productive to show you that there are better ways to talk about this. Anyway, America found out about Florida because Juan Ponce de León invaded it and America felt like all that cane sugar and swampland and capacity to run rum should belong to America, and so then it did, because the President sent a group from Georgia to wage a guerilla war against the local governments and gain an American foothold. Which worked! At some point the President, when he was still the Secretary of State and just before becoming the President, called Florida "a derelict open to the occupancy of every enemy, civilized or savage, of the United States, and serving no other earthly purpose than as a post of annoyance to them." Soon after, Spain fled

Florida, considering it to be a burden. So now all America had to do was do a genocide on all the Seminoles, who had given home and safety to runaway slaves, so that in the 1960s, the CIA, having been invented by America in 1947, could decide that it would make a lot of sense to use its resources to find a way to make sure that Florida voters could not in any way interfere with the Walt Disney Company's efforts to buy up vast amounts of land at a very cheap price and construct a massive theme park. This worked out great!

A survey shows that Americans are, on the whole, surprised by abuses of power.

Today at work, lunch is provided during the meeting everyone has to attend. It is tacos. It is Tuesday. Sam is on his phone but so is everyone else. There is a sound in the air nobody can recognize. Outside is a single plane, circling. Soon, other planes join, maybe three or four. No one's noticed this yet but to be fair, they've been in a meeting, all throughout Manhattan (it's Tuesday, what else was going to happen on a Tuesday?) and anyway now the meeting's over, and Sam goes to the window. Sam hears a sound he absolutely does not recognize. He looks down at the street, then up at the sky. Sam texts Eleanor, *are there planes circling?* and Eleanor texts him back, *????*, so Sam sends her a photo. *Weird*, she texts him. Eleanor does not get up to go to the windows. Not yet, anyway. Marks comes over. Yes, his name is Marks, that's not a typo, no I don't understand it, even though I'm the narrator. "What's up?" asks Marks. "Planes are circling," says Sam. "Oh," says Marks. "Yeah," says Marks. "Wow," says Marks. "There must be nearly ten or something," says Julie, who has just now appeared, with a tiny cup of salsa she is eating with a spoon. Sam, at the window, moves his finger through the air, counts nine, ten, twelve, "Weird!" says Betty, at the other end of the very long, slightly narrow office lined, head to toe, with windows. "How many planes are there?" "Twenty maybe?" Maybe twenty planes are circling over Manhattan. There's a weird low sound. "Does anyone hear that?" Nobody answers. "Does anyone know what's going on?" Sam goes into the lobby and hits the button for an elevator, which shows up, and Sam gets into the elevator, and sticks his leg out to hold the door open, because everyone knows an elevator door will never close on a limb and plummet to the ground with your limb out there like that getting torn asunder, and he cranes his neck around to wait for the little TV inside the elevator that shouts the news to cycle through to the air traffic portion. There's bound to be an air traffic portion, Sam has sworn he's seen it before, an air traffic notice on the little TV inside the elevator, tiny planes swirling around. Sam thinks about how insane it is that there are little TVs in the elevator when his cellphone doesn't even have service in the elevator, *I* think it's insane that they have TVs in the elevator, the news wasn't even really certain what they were talking about anymore, and, anyway, the elevator monitor doesn't seem to have an air traffic portion. Something like thirty or forty planes are circling over Manhattan. It is increasingly ominous. That weird sound is still there. Across town, Eleanor heads to the window, looks to the sky, and immediately goes back to her desk, picks up her bag, and heads home. As we turn on the news, the news is saying, LOOK OUTSIDE IT'S A BEAUTIFUL DAY, and everyone looks outside, and the sky is full of planes, and the news says, THAT'S ALL THERE IS TO SAY ABOUT THAT, and so they turn off the news. Sam took out his phone and checked if anyone had seen anything. Eleanor is sitting on the train. She hasn't looked up in almost an hour. She sent an email confirming she'll work from home. All through the city, nobody seems to know what's going on, but everyone is being assured it's fine. THIS IS FINE, says the news, IT IS NOTHING TO WORRY ABOUT. EVENTUALLY SOMETHING ELSE WILL HAPPEN. JUST BE HAPPY THINGS SEEM TO BE WORKING OUT, STOP ASKING ME QUESTIONS. There are fifty planes overhead. Hours have passed. Everyone is standing at the window, eating their three thirty snacks. Nobody seems to know what else to do. The planes are still circling. The sky is full of them now. I mean it. *Saw the planes, went home,* texted Eleanor to Sam. They've choked the sky. Their engines fill the air with an untenable roaring. It's the only sound there is. Your whole life is a dull and endless roar, with no explanation ever made available. Certain doom has your past six residences, and is trying them all. Imagine being in the air and circling Manhattan for hours, imagine seeing all the planes out your window, seeing the people inside the planes outside the window, imagine just see-ing yourself in every single plane, imagine it, now. Meanwhile, "Is that the sound from earlier?" asks Marks. "No," says Sam. "No it isn't." Sam leaves the office. It has nothing more to give him, today. He texts Eleanor, *i love you,* while all around, the entire city is staring at the sky, choked with planes. Sam's on the train, and then he's off the train. So much time passes.

It's hardly worth mentioning. Eleanor has texted Sam to meet her at the place down the street from their apartment and barely a block from the train that has frozen dark and stormies, and whose happy hour special is $10 and consists of three jerk chicken wings, a bottle of Red Stripe, and a shot of dark rum. The sun is setting. Their neighbors are everywhere, and the landlords are nowhere to be seen. Tomorrow Sam will go get a haircut. Today he can pay for both of their drinks. Tonight they'll watch a movie and go to sleep. In the middle of the night, Eleanor will wake up. She'll look over at Sam. "Sam," she'll say. Sam will hold her for the rest of the night. She breathes, slowly, in his arms, as she settles back into sleep.

Sam and Eleanor are on the couch, watching that movie where a widowed bookkeeper goes to the opera with a horny baker, an aged Sicilian woman almost dies but ultimately does not, a woman curses a plane with mixed results, a Brooklyn couple gets some expensive plumbing work done, a husband treats his wife poorly though he loves her, an old man walks his dogs and feeds them people food, a college professor is invited to have a nice dinner with a woman his own age and afterwards walks her home, two kind and affectionate grocery clerks worry about a bank deposit for like twenty minutes, and, overhead, the moon looms, large, at all times, ruining lives and drowning whole cities.

July in New York is hot. It's ridiculous. August is also awful, but August comes after July, so you're sort of ready for it, but

July comes out of nowhere. Eighty-six to 102 is a threat, every single building is covered in glass. Your power bill will destroy you so you don't dare to turn on the stove so you order out and then it turns out ordering out will destroy you so you live with destruction. Sam and Eleanor bought a second air conditioner so that the window unit from the bedroom could live forever in the living room which was also the kitchen and the new air conditioner, mobile and based on the floor, could live wherever. May the good Lord bless and keep their two salaries for all their days. Every day Sam and Eleanor got up and went to work and ate lunch and they texted about what they would do for dinner and one of them would get the groceries for dinner and Sam would cook them dinner and then they would sit down with their favorite Italian American family that was definitely a member of the mob until the screen went black and the story was over and they came out of it changed, in their own ways.

Eleanor said to Sam, "Can you save $2,000," and Sam panicked and then after catching his breath said, "Uhhh eventually, eventually I could do that," and Eleanor said, "Great," and Sam said, "Why?" and Eleanor said, "So we can open an account together instead of keeping track of who got groceries, we just put money in it regularly and use it to go to the movies and get groceries and go on vacation and not ever worry about how we're splitting it because we already split it because we made this together and it's ours and it's for us and also we can pay rent with it instead of paying each other, and it'll have our names on it, bound for glory." "I long," said

Sam, "to be glory-bound." "I know you do, baby," said Eleanor. Sam was sitting down. He wrapped his arms around
Eleanor. He would figure out a way to set aside $2,000 to
build a better future for them. He had absolutely no idea how
this would work but he would figure it out. One day they
would be bound for glory. The world would be a promise that
someone could keep. The clouds would part and the angels
would come, with their billion eyes, their many wings, their
fiery swords, their language that is beyond our ears and limbs.

It's possible we should talk about the angels. They're not in
the room so it's OK. So when we think about angels we seem
to tend think of them as being beautiful, and wingéd, and
they are!, but let's be clear: celestial geometry has nothing
at all to do with the human body and its coffin-like confines.
This is the box we are born into and will die in, and angels are
beyond language and sight, an incomprehensible geometry of
eyes and wings, their flaming sword of judgment, God's divine wrath, a miracle of doom, it ain't even a sword, just a
judgment to spit from a mouth you did not have upon the
lives of everyone downstairs on earth you were charged with
sitting in judgment of. The other thing I want to be clear on
is that, at the end, the angels finally come. Wouldn't you like
to be there?

And then, suddenly, and without warning, all across America,
it was time for dinner.

This was the summer where no big movies came out, no small movies came out, where honestly no movies came out, where all you could see was the same February dumps but they never left, they just played over and over and over until the fall came, bringing with it glad tidings and new movies, and to this day no explanation has been offered. It was the summer of fried chicken tacos and white people discovering how to make elote at home. It was easy and it was beautiful and if you had a cast iron skillet it was even better. To claim it was anything other than pretty much totally inauthentic would be a lie but if it's the best you can do it doesn't make it taste less good. Basically mix a half cup of mayo and three-quarters of a cup of cotija with sour cream or full-fat Greek yogurt and like a quarter cup of lime juice and a teaspoon of, ideally, ancho chili powder, or the nearest thing you can get, and toss the corn you tossed in a cast iron with that. It's delicious. Maybe have it with a fried chicken taco with a little lettuce, tomato, and cheese. This was the summer where nobody could leave the house for two weeks because it was so hot you would die, and everyone who could not get to air conditioning in time actually did die and their bodies were piled on the street until one day they weren't. It was the summer when the secret police played the exact same song that ice-cream trucks play, and after that nobody saw their children ever again. People had to have more children because there weren't any left and it was impossible to get birth control of any sort without a prescription and prescriptions for birth control were, technically, illegal. How do we look at all of this and open our hearts, every day, to love? I'm asking because I need to know. I really and truly need to know. My heart is breaking every single day.

It's hot today. It's too hot to go to the beach because at the beach, in this heat, you will boil inside your own skin like a lobster or a hot dog within ten seconds, the sun is so huge that no umbrella could ever cover you, and not even the ocean will try to save you, so thank God for the air conditioners conditioning the air towards a state we can try to live inside of! For dinner Sam is going to make something that reminds him of summer. It is not Eleanor's favorite, but he has a plan. Anyway dinner is some mahi-mahi cooked on a grill pan, frozen corn kernels cooked in butter with salt and basil and pepper, and white rice with a little lime and butter, but the most important thing is that Sam has gone into the office and closed the door. Eleanor is in the bedroom, far from here, reading by the window. Outside it is so hot that the cars, who are parked, become alarmed. A man is walking through the neighborhood dragging a speaker the size of a suitcase behind him. So far everything he's done has made things better. Who among us can claim the same?

Sam laid down a plastic tarp in the office. On top of the plastic tarp he inflated a kiddie pool, which he has filled with water. He put sand around the kiddie pool, and there are folding chairs too. There's a cooler of drinks. He has Italian ices in the freezer. He tells Eleanor to put on her bathing suit and she says, "Why," and he says, "I don't ask that much of you!" and she sighs, and figures *fine*, she looks good in the bathing suit, she likes it, she hasn't gotten to wear it in a bit, and she opens the door to the office.

Sam took the beach to Eleanor. They opened the window and a truly terrible heat came through. But this is how it is at the beach. They closed the office door. It was Saturday. Nobody had anywhere to be. Sam had put all the computers and monitors in the closet, he taped the closet door shut. There is no way to know if this is a good idea in the context of being a renter, but I can tell you with absolute certainty that it is a wonderful thing to do for someone you love in the summertime.

Italian ice is amazing, though it's absolutely best in Philadelphia, where it's known as water (/wʊdːər/) ice. Either way, it's probably derived from granita, an Italian dessert which you can make using fresh fruit (cubed), lemon or lime juice, some sugar, some salt, and a freezer. Basically you blend the fruit with the juice and sugar and then the salt, then you freeze it in a shallow pan for maybe forty-five minutes. Then you take it out of the freezer and scrape it up with a fork to break up the chunks, then put it back in the freezer for like maybe four hours. If you have too much fruit and don't want to go out, this is a great thing to do. The secret police could be anywhere, really. So make some granita this summer!

OK so it's 1956. J. Edgar Hoover, the head of the Federal Bureau of Investigation, which he basically invented, invents COINTELPRO, a domestic counterintelligence program which carries out a series of covert and illegal projects to destroy and discredit organizations the FBI deems subversive, like the civil rights movement, feminists, feminism, antiwar organizers, environmentalists, American Indians, proponents of Puerto Rican independence, and the KKK. In their eyes, these groups are, apparently, identical. In 1971, COINTEL-PRO financed, armed, and directed the attacks of a group of right-wing terrorists, who referred to themselves as the Secret Army Organization. Yes it's weird that they convinced right-wing terrorists to do executions for the state, assuming you think the state wants you anything but shackled and dying of debt. All of this was, more or less, authorized by the President of the United States, who figured, every one of them, and often independently!, that America would be a better place if people didn't object to things so much.

When I die, I want to be buried
in a boat, and I want that
boat to be floated out onto the
lake in Prospect Park, at sunset,
by the boathouse, and then I want
that boat to be set on fire. I'm
putting this here so people can
know my wishes. Thanks in advance!

SAM WENT ON THE INTERNET and asked if anyone knew what was up with all those planes circling Manhattan the other day, and he waits for his answers, but his answers never come, and Eleanor asks him what he's doing and he tells her, "I am waiting for the good people of the internet to gift me with answers," and Eleanor stops for a minute, and she waits too. Sam's question is gone now. "It was probably blackbagged," says Eleanor, and she's right. They both get very quiet. They wonder what they should delete from their phones. They sit for a very long time, thinking about this. They don't come up with any answers. Eventually they nudge each other to bed. They forget to brush their teeth, to wash their faces, their clothes are on the floor, they're laying in bed, they're under the covers, with all of their fears, and their hopes, and their dreams. Tomorrow will be different, whisper the secret police. All across America, the sun sets, and it rises. In Germany they paid reparations for the Holocaust, they put up memorials to the dead to remind everyone of the horrors they hope to never repeat. Here we have 240 schools named after Confederate leaders, who declared war on the government because they felt it was their God-given right to enslave and rape and murder and brutalize an entire race, to strip them of their homes and their hopes and their families and their dreams, because it was cheaper than paying someone a fair day's wage to work. I just want to know how tomorrow is going to be any different if we still can't agree on what happened yesterday over three hundred years later. You know?

Good night! Sleep tight! Beware the secret police! I love you with all my heart!

Eleanor's away all week on a team-building exercise. It's some sort of summer camp situation. There're bunks, and tennis courts, and a pool, and cookouts, and team-building exercises about synergy, and also branding. It's been two days. Sam is not a fan of this! Secretly, neither is Eleanor. But, also secretly, she's a little glad to get out of the city, and out of their apartment, and just sort of clear her head out here, in the landscape, with its synergy, and its branding, and its poolside luaus. When Eleanor thinks about Sam she swears she can see his heart beating in his chest, clear as day, and crowned in flames. Sam's sitting at his desk, where his heart, beating in his chest, is crowned in flames. Sam misses Eleanor. He hates sleeping alone, he hates that the bed is so empty without Eleanor, and it's a queen bed which is always much bigger than he's used to when no one else is there, and anyway Sam has to go to a meeting. He'll be back soon! Eleanor calls Sam, but he doesn't answer. *Fuck Sam*, thinks Eleanor. She smiles at a coworker, across the pool, who she has never seen before. Eleanor thinks about sending Sam a nude. The day keeps going. Sam finds a really cool menorah on sale online. It'll look great in the apartment, and it'll surprised Eleanor. Now that Sam has finally accomplished something today, he can go home and cook dinner. He marinated a pork chop in a mustardy Carolina barbecue sauce and, after firing up the rice cooker, he skins and chops a real big carrot and puts it and a fat pat of butter in some olive oil in a pan. After that he tosses the pork chop in a skillet. He gets out maple syrup and dried lemon peel and salt and pepper and he salts and peppers the chop and once the chop starts searing he tosses some dried lemon peel on the carrots and then adds a bit of maple syrup and covers that pan. You need to do the carrots first because they will take a little longer than the chop depending of course on how thick the chop is, and Sam did get a bone-in chop, and thank God he already started the rice. I know this is kind of like a few other things, and I'm sorry! Sometimes Sam runs out of ideas for what to cook and he goes back to things he finds comforting, which he tends to also want to fall back on, for comfort, when Eleanor is gone. I promise, I hope, that he'll make something different tomorrow. Sam makes himself a mezcal old-fashioned with some sugar and some lemon and orange and grapefruit bitters. It's nice. He sits down on the couch and stretches out without her. He texts Eleanor. He gave her a flash drive full of movies before she left, so that, if she wanted, at night, they could call each other up, on speaker, and watch the same movie. This would be sweeter if she was going to be gone longer than a week. It's still a little sweet, at least. Sam gets into bed. He sends Eleanor a photo of himself, in bed. Good night, Sam! In bed, Eleanor and Sam like to look at each other's faces before they sleep. They'll try to look at each other's faces when they wake up. It's been incredibly important to them, that they are the first and the last thing the other sees every day. The rest of the day can be whatever it wants, a day is, generally, just a day. You work. You have lunch. You go back to work. Sometimes a very strange thing happens, like a single cloud falls from the sky and sits in the street, filling the windows, or your coworker secretly turns out to be a government agent, or suddenly the Mayor declares that all leases are month-to-month now, and you periodically need to suddenly pack up and find a new home whenever someone is willing to pay more for your apartment than you

are, it's fun, it's fine, and it's deeply relatable, sometimes you
miss the light of your life, sometimes you get lonely, sometimes the sky falls right on the floor and then there it is, on the
floor. Sam, at home, turns on his video game, and tries to find
out if this is when, finally, the angels come. Sam finds Eleanor.
Eleanor is sitting in her bunk bed adorned with festive lights.
It's really beautiful. He loves her so much. Eleanor, sitting in
her bunk bed adorned with festive lights, misses Sam. She
thinks about how she is probably getting a raise after this.
Then she thinks about how, a year ago, Sam was barely employed, and now they had two stable incomes, they could go
out to dinner anytime if they wanted, so long as it wasn't
more than once or twice a week, they could save up, together,
start a checking account together that they could use for groceries and rent and the movies and dinner, that they could use
to more easily build a life together, meanwhile Sam wonders
if he is sad, and lost. Sam really tries to think of something
else. Tomorrow night, even though it's summer, Sam will run
all the air conditioners (this is after he prepares a large quan-
tity of a very very light salad of butter lettuce with cracked
pepper and salt and olive oil, I mean really good olive oil, and
breakfast of a demi baguette with butter from the bakery
downstairs from his office which smells so incredible, all of
the time) because tomorrow night Sam is going to make his
gorgonzola browned-butter alfredo, which he never does anymore, because Eleanor is extremely lactose intolerant, which
is why they have switched to oat milk, and he desperately
hopes he can remember the ratios. Anyway that's what Sam
will do tomorrow, he decides, as Eleanor calls. "Tomorrow
night I'm going to make alfredo," says Sam. "In the summer?"

says Eleanor. "In the summer," says Sam. "Sam, I love you very, very much." "I love you too! With all my heart." Sometimes we sleep through the night, and sometimes lunch is catered. Those are always great days. At the team-building retreat, lunch is *always* catered. Eleanor will text Sam pictures of the meals. It is as much a gesture of love as it is a tender sort of taunt. The future of websites is up for discussion, the shopping cart is yours for the taking. The new interface will change your life, in that it might actually, this time, work. It would be great if the government could afford this so that their websites worked but either the websites can work or we can invent a new kind of missile that also kills Muslims, we absolutely cannot do both, and which would you rather have, an easy way to access your medications and pay your taxes, or dead Muslims? Eleanor may actually lose her mind this week. No one's making any promises. When Sam gets home, the angels are there. Sam stays with the angels for so long that he forgets all about dinner. I know! What the fuck! Don't worry though, Sam has just remembered about dinner. He orders a pizza. Last night he made the alfredo, it's been a while, but, I think it's like two parts cream to one part butter, you brown the butter and toss in like two to four minced cloves of garlic, then you remove from heat and whisk in the cream, you bring the temp back up, you add in gorgonzola and some parmesan, you crack some black pepper in there, you roast broccoli, you sauté some chicken maybe in white wine vinegar and black pepper, you bring water to a boil, you boil the pasta in the water, you plate it, it's delicious, I swear to God. This is how time passes when you're alone! One day it's tomorrow and then tomorrow's yesterday, and here comes the pizza. Eleanor was in meetings. She cannot wait to call Sam and tell him all about them. The pizza arrives, and Eleanor calls. Some things just work out. In the morning, Sam gets up. Sam goes to work. Eleanor rolls out of the bunk bed adorned with festive lights, and she showers. She has invested in pajamas that double as clothing. They are linen, she is salaried, and Sam is in a meeting where he's thinking about money, which nobody can ever have enough of. Where are the angels? The angels are in Heaven. Where is Sam? Sam is heading home, where he will make a caprese pasta with cherry tomatoes, mozzarella, cavatappi, and pesto. Sam, right now, lets the pasta cool before tossing in the mozzarella. It's a really really pleasant summer dish. He has a bottle of pét-nat. Sam's letting everything chill. Where's Eleanor? Eleanor is sitting at the pool for happy hour. Where are the secret police? It's a secret! But that coworker she's never seen before is winking at her.

He comes over.

The coworker has a beard, well-trimmed, and his hair's dark and cropped close and receding but *not* thinning, and he comes over, and he, the coworker no one has ever seen before, says, "Hi." Eleanor's about to say, "Hi! I have a boyfriend, I'm sorry, I know I smiled at you so now you think I'm going to fuck you, but it wasn't even you I was smiling at, it was the idea of you, which was just anything other than what I had, which was a thought I felt like entertaining for like ten seconds but not in a serious way, and now you're here, and it'd be best, probably, if we both did a shot and then walked away and never looked at each other again!" and then she says it, and he says, "You misunderstand. I'm a government agent. Would you like to foil some terrorists?" and she says, "What kind of terrorists?" and he says "Muslims," and she says, "No thank you!" and he says, "Why not don't you love your country?" and Eleanor tells him, "Mostly yes, but honestly, I thought you'd say those white supremacists, hiding over there in that van, with their assault rifles, and white robes, preparing to go murder everyone in that black Baptist church down the road." "Oh," says the government agent, "Those aren't terrorists, they're just a little misguided." And so Eleanor says, "Excuse me," and gets up, and he gets up, and Eleanor trips him so he falls in the pool, and, as he falls, she grabs his gun from his belt and puts it in the pocket of her robe, which she is wearing, and begins to hoof it across the field of the resort. She reaches the fence and vaults it. She reaches the van and shoots a white supremacist in the head. There's another inside the van. He tries to start the van, but it misfires, and she gets him through the eye. Eleanor wipes the gun, and drops it. In America what's so great is that if you have enough money you can buy someone's debt from the bank and then make money off of their debt which tends to drive them further into debt and then you can make money of *that*, which is *especially* great. Making money is the best! The van, meanwhile, erupts into flames. Eleanor is headed home to her man, Sam, and his heart on fire. This would be a good time for the angels to come. But that time isn't now, because Eleanor's home!

"Baby!" says Sam, "you're home early!" "Yes I am! I missed you so much I had to come right home to you, and it was for no other reasons! I love you!" And she does!!! She kisses him right on the mouth, which is on the front of his face. She puts her hand on his chest over his heart, which is right there, and beating, and crowned in flames. Sam pours her some pét-nat and gets them both bowls of the caprese pasta. Eleanor says, "I missed you," and Sam says, "I missed you." Eleanor shouts, "I missed you!" and then Sam, with his mouth full!, shouts, "I missed you!" "I missed you so much!" said Sam, because he did! And Eleanor stood up and looked him in the eye until the world ended.

What's that? You want to hear more about labor relations in America?

A wildcat strike is when the members of a union strike without prior authorization from their union's leadership. They've been illegal in America since 1935. Now if union membership believes that their union's leadership is not adequately representing their interests, then they can petition the National Labor Relations Board to formally end their association with their union, and then a wildcat strike is no longer illegal, because it is no longer unauthorized by union leadership, because there would then be no union leadership to not authorize it. This does sometimes open up what we could call a whole new can of worms if, say, American businesses were still into hiring people to go around and kill and discredit American civilians to keep the herds in line. Sam has watched the entire history of labor relations in America unfold in his game. Angels can move throughout all time, eventually. They can watch anything that has ever happened. It is possible that they can watch anything that ever *will* happen, but Sam has, for personal reasons, always been a little nervous about the concept of the future.

Sam had at this point maybe $630 in the savings account Eleanor had asked him to think about opening. It was so much more than he thought he'd have, but it's so much less than he was supposed to have. I'm not going to pretend Eleanor was thrilled at Sam's lack of progress at saving $2,000. Eleanor was not thrilled. She wanted Sam to think about their future, and to commit to it together. Living costs money, and it's fucking awful!

"Sam," said Eleanor, "you have a job now. You have a good job, and they value you even if they don't understand you, and they keep paying you! I don't understand why you can't do this. I don't understand why this is so hard. I love you so much, Sam, and I want us to work towards a future together, to build a life for ourselves, and I know this is hard, I know money makes you feel fucked up, but we have to do this!"

Sam knows! He knows this! But here's the thing, he feels: "I spent *years* living on the poverty line. I have $10,000 worth of credit card debt from buying my groceries, from sometimes buying drinks, from trying to not feel poor, from trying to not be seen as poor. And it's hard! I have $300 a month in credit card payments, just to make the minimum, and I probably get charged $195 a month in interest, and I have maybe $400 a month in student loan payments, and my half of the rent is

$1,175, and that's almost one check, and we go out, we buy things for the apartment, we have a beautiful life! And it's fucked because I know how good an idea this is, and I want to do it so badly, and I find it so hard. I find it so hard to not spend the money I have when I have it, to think about money as something that will always be there, it's so hard somehow to know that I know that the next check is in two weeks, every two weeks, forever, basically. And I don't know why I don't know that yet. And I'm sorry."

Did I ever tell you that, back when he was un- to barely employed, Sam made $50 a month too much to qualify for the Supplemental Nutrition Assistance Program, or what people call food stamps? SNAP gives you $204 a month for groceries at the first of every month, and he made $50 too much to save $204 a month.

Did I ever tell you how often Eleanor cried herself to sleep about this? How, when they were first dating, the nights she and Sam didn't spend together, she'd think about his life, and weep? To see him struggling so hard to make rent, to pay for a date, to see the way he'd scrape a budget together to cover the most basic things, things she'd never needed to worry about? It broke her heart in fucking half! She thought about how much she loved him and about how little she could stop this from hurting him, and she wept. She did everything she could. She'd slip small bills into his wallet when he was asleep or cooking them dinner. She'd hold him all night during the few hours he managed to sleep. Was this a fight? Were they fighting about money? No. Eleanor was confused why this couldn't be a priority for Sam, and Sam was confused as to why Eleanor didn't understand in her bones how scared he

was of money, and she did, she did understand how scared
he was, but she also couldn't feel that fear, it wasn't in her
bones. They were scared in different ways about the future,
and that felt weird, and new. I don't think it's a bad thing, is
what Sam said. "I don't think it's a bad thing. I think I have to
be better. I think you have to be a little more patient. I think
I have to outline a budget I can stick to. I think I thought
because I had money I didn't need to worry about money, but
you always need to worry about money. There's no such thing
as enough money, that's the whole point of money, that it's
never enough." "Sam, I love you so much" "I love you with
absolutely everything I have," "Are you sure this isn't a fight?
We're both crying and raising our voices," "Eleanor, we love
to cry and raise our voices," "OK fair point," "I do think it's
a bad thing that I haven't done enough to save, and I think it's
not a good thing that you're not being patient enough with me,
but I think, like, we both have pains and fears, and to find out
they're not always the same isn't a bad thing, it just means we
can see this better now," "We can build these bridges," "To
each other and to the future," "Together," "Until the world
ends," "And we're nothing but light."

Nothing but light! Imagine! Imagine being nothing but light,
with a million eyes, and a flaming sword, and wings beyond
description! Imagine never being afraid of money, imagine
never walking away from love, imagine how nice it would
be if the things we dreamed of were something other than
dreams! Wouldn't that really be something? In Heaven are the
angels, on Earth are the people, in the banks is the money, in

our hearts are our hopes and dreams, in their homes are the landlords, on the street are the unhoused, in the graves are the bodies and their bones and their hopes and their dreams, and the secret police are everywhere, and the air is full of ghosts. Tonight, before bed, we'll check the locks, like we always do and, because it's Sunday, we'll tell each other our hopes and dreams for the week. I can't make you any promises other than that I love you. I don't know that this world will allow me to keep a single one. But I love you. I love you so much.

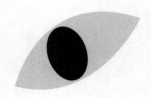

Meanwhile, it's fall.

OK SO IT'S 1582. Pope Gregory XIII changed the calendar from the Julian to the Gregorian, because of some trouble with leap years, which is what happens when you live on a rotating body orbiting a sun, I just mean it's insane to expect things to continue to be the same from one day to the next, anyway, on October 4, 1582, the Julian calendar ended and on October 15, 1582, the Gregorian calendar started. Jews sit shiva for a week because it took the good Lord seven days to create the world and each life lost is a world the sun will never rise on again. Pretty much all societies at one point or another believed that the purpose of birds was to carry the souls of the dead to Heaven, which is why New York has so many pigeons. It's raining today and it has been all week. Tomorrow the clouds will part for the first time in days, and we, along with all the plants in the apartment, will be bathed in light.

All the leaves are beautiful and then they're dead. Every tree is a gift and then the sidewalk's a grave. But here's the thing! Everything dies! That's a fact! But right now everyone is wearing sweaters. Everyone looks beautiful in a sweater. They're soft and mysterious. So I don't know what the problem is. The air at night gets to be the sort of cold that hurts just a little if you breathe too deep. It is more than enough to remind you that you're alive. The sun starts to set earlier than you'd like but in the meantime you have a drink, and the moon is always there, at the window, and gawking. When fall hits you get to bury summer. You hide your air conditioners for months. The power bill is reborn as both miracle and blessing. All around you the world is holding its breath. Are you really telling me you don't want to see what happens next?

It's Halloween and the President has turned the White House into the haunted White House. It is full of ghosts. It is choking on them! They are spilling out the windows. They are screaming for justice. But nobody can hear them, because they're dead. It's pretty hard to hear ghosts! On the lawn he has arranged the bodies of everyone who has died during his term.

In fall, the sun starts setting between seven and six, which is just enough time for Sam and Eleanor to both be home on a Friday night to light the candles and say the words to welcome rest into their lives. Tonight the entire apartment is full of flowers. You can barely breathe. It's so beautiful. The candles are out. Come here. Please. Yes. Just like that.

Eleanor sits in a big brass bed. She removes all of her clothes. She stands on top of the bed. She tears the world down around her. She wreaks her vengeance. She orders dinner. She stays like that for days.

Across the street, there's a woman looking at a man over and over again because the longer you look at an object the more likely you are to feel something and what she feels is her chest turning into the sun and her whole body burns up with light, it's spilling out her eyes and her mouth; next there's a baby; now there's a ghost. Across the street way out in America there's a rental car reassembled in the yard, the clouds part, the Cuyahoga remains on fire, our prayers mean nothing, Jane's moved to Cleveland, Isabella's in her castle, the orchestra's back in Berlin, with Johnny, who will one day die, Geronimo is tutoring privately, the secret police are hiding in your dreams, that's why you can't find them, or your dreams. Last night we all went to the same bar and ordered different drinks and when we went to the bathroom we walked out of our skins. Last night a cop pulled a car over. All the lights were gone and we were blanketed in darkness. When this is over, we won't even have our bones.

Did you forget about the secret police? You did, didn't you. It's OK, I get it, you probably don't know anyone who got blackbagged, the only people you'll never see again are the people you got to say goodbye to, and that's incredible! But, hey. Maybe don't forget about the secret police. Because they're everywhere. And they don't need a reason to come for you, and they don't need a warrant, they'll just throw you into a black bag, and then toss that black bag you're in into a van, and then nobody ever sees you, ever again. I absolutely have no idea what happens after you go into the van. I think about it all the time. It's fucking terrifying to me. ANYWAY, says the news, BACK TO THE STORY!

OK so it's 1991. Imagine a little boy. He's in a blue-and-white striped bathing suit, one of those ones that could be housing a diaper, his face is mostly cheeks and concern, he's in too-wide rain boots as big as his legs and a yellow raincoat with the hood fallen back, one of those rubber ones that sticks to you in the sort of humidity headed our way with a vengeance and a motive and a very clear window of opportunity, he's standing at the edge of the river, at the bank, he's looking in. He can't see anything. He wants to lean in but sees himself falling, in, and being swallowed up by an enormous carp with terrible teeth and no purpose at all in this life except to be a carp and to swallow this poor boy. So he doesn't lean in. He studies the water, all cheeks and concern in his raincoat that will soon stick to him, uncomfortably. The surface of the water is disturbing. I mean it's being disturbed. A carp rises up. Its head is the size of the boy. It's enormous. The boy knows that this carp is a carp that grants wishes. He just knows it. The carp admits it can grant wishes, *I can grant wishes, how did you know?*, and asks the boy how he knew this. The boy just looks at the carp. The carp's head is entirely out of the water, but the rest of its body is beneath the water. It could be crouching. It could have the body of a bear, or a boy, crouching under all that water. We just don't really know anything about this carp. The carp asks the boy if it's his birthday soon. *It's your birthday soon, isn't it.* The boy understands that this isn't really a question. The carp waits for the boy to make a wish. It just sits there. In his heart is a wish. He holds it so close it almost dies. The carp tells him that that was the wrong wish. *That's the wrong wish*, says the carp. The carp is enormous now. It's almost touching the boy. The carp urges the boy to try again. He can see the slick mucus on the scales bending the light around him. *That's the wrong wish*, says the carp. It's even bigger now, somehow. The boy's the size of its mouth now, can smell its wet gut. *Once more*, says the carp, *with feeling*. The boy collapses with feeling. The carp's gone. The boy's up. The window was opened, now here's the humidity. His coat is part of his skin now. He's up, and the last thing he remembers is terrifying, and now his raincoat is part of his skin! He cries out and tries to tear it off, but it's his skin now. He looks around, tears streaming down his face, but nobody's coming to help him! He is all alone! He screams, and then tries to swallow it. Time passes. Birds circle over his head. There was a light. Now it's dimmed. He stops crying, in increments, and tries to adjust the rubber raincoat so it sticks less bad. He heads home and hopes the weather fixes something between here and there. At home it's a birthday party, it's the little boy's birthday party, all his friends and family are assembled, he's opening the first present, he just can't wait, he tugs the bow, and it's wrapped in this way that when the bow's pulled, with a violent sort of grace, the wrapping comes off clean and the box tumbles open, and in the box is the floating head of the dog that pursues him, slowly, in his dreams, and it looks him in the eye, and it opens its mouth, and it's the sound of a siren, it's screaming, it's a warning, it's not in time, it's too late, and they're all gone, and it's terrible.

Sam wants to make stew for dinner. Sam emails his boss and asks if he can work from home. Sam does not hear back and gets on the train. Halfway to work Sam gets service and, with

the service, the OK. Sam gets off the train and walks across
the platform to the Brooklyn-bound train which is, just now,
pulling into the station. Sam thanks his boss. Nobody is sure
who he answers to and nobody wants to tell him no. Sam
gets two to three OK bottles of red and two or more pounds
of a roast. He immediately goes home and cuts the roast into
one inch cubes and marinates this in red wine and soy sauce.
Sam opens up his computer and checks his email. He gets his
calls forwarded to his cell. Nobody has asked a single thing of
him yet, so he goes to the store and gets a package of bacon,
a sack of carrots, several Yukon golds, a package of naked
garlic cloves (you know, peeled garlic cloves, it's absolutely so
much easier than shelling and peeling the cloves, and it's so
much better than those jars of minced and preserved garlic,
it's fresher, anyway), and some shallots. Sam cooks the package of bacon in his five-quart Dutch oven. His phone shouts
that there's an email. Someone wants to come into the office
to do a presentation and will provide lunch. Sam forwards
the email to the office and requires them to answer a poll.
While the office reads and answers, Sam reserves the bacon,
for later. He covers the pot. He did not marinate the beef
long enough but here we are. Yes, this is basically a bour-
guignon, except Sam hates mushrooms. Sam sears the beef
in the bacon fat while salting and peppering, vigorously. He
turns the beef. He does not crowd the pot. Once seared he
removes the beef's cubes, cooking in batches till they're done.
He skins and chops the carrots and tosses them in the bacon
fat while reducing the heat to low. He chops the shallots into
rings and coarsely chops the garlic. He tosses in the shallots
and waits a bit to toss in the garlic. He immediately chops the

potatoes into beef-sized chunks and tosses them in there too. He salts this and peppers this and stirs. He waits a little for the potatoes to get starchy, and as soon as it looks like they are he tosses the beef back in. The beef is browning more now, and everything smells amazing. The Cuyahoga River has not stopped burning. Sam plugs in the slow cooker and removes the Dutch oven from heat. Things can burn in the Dutch oven, but they don't in the slow cooker, and Sam has to work! He salts and peppers again and throws in thyme and sage. He puts in a bottle of wine and a cup of beef stock and three or more tablespoons of tomato paste. He puts in five tablespoons of tomato paste. Sorry. He lets this stew for at least four hours. He works. Out the window is a bus. In the sky is the moon and so is the sun. Sam texts Eleanor to pick up a very good baguette. *Would a perfectly good baguette also work?* A perfectly good baguette would also work. Sam writes and answers several emails. Eleanor comes home. Sam tosses the bacon in a pan to crisp it a bit, then he crumbles it. That goes on top of the stew. The bread's still warm. Sam pours them some wine.

"No. Don't move. Stay there. I mean it! Jesus just, yes, stay right there. Don't move! I swear to God if you move. Not yet. Not yet! OK. Yes. OK. OK. Thank you. Thank you. Jesus. Thank you."

This was all happening during a period of time people kept referring to as *late capitalism*, as though this implied it might be over soon.

People died so we could have a forty-hour workweek. People died so we could have a forty-hour workweek. I just really really need you to remember that people died so we could have a forty-hour workweek. They died in Haymarket Square and they died in Everett, Washington, and they died in the mines and they died in the mills and they died at the hands of the Pinkertons hired to put down the strikes at any cost and the cost was human lives, which are worth infinitely less than, it turns out, money. I just need you to never, ever forget, every second you work, that people died so we could have a forty-hour workweek. This morning, the moon was low in the sky in Prospect Park. Clouds lined the treetops. An eight-hour day was once worth dying for. The moon is everywhere. You couldn't escape it if you tried.

Really, I don't know what you're hoping for, but I hope that this is it.

OK so it's 1569. False flag operations have been invented by the Oxford English Dictionary and have honestly only gained in popularity. At the time, a false flag operation was a purely figurative expression for when you like deliberately misrepresented someone's opinions or motives, and then it was when, in naval battles, ships would fly the enemy's flag to get up close before blasting the shit out of them with cannons and such as that (it's funny that what started as a figurative expression became a literal act, right? Jokes are funny when you point them out, right? I've got a real good joke for you later,

I swear), and then (and now!) a false flag was an act "committed with the intent of disguising the actual source of responsibility and pinning blame on a second party." Like, say, Pilgrims dressing up as Natives and killing other Pilgrims to get the rest of the Pilgrims to turn against the Natives, who housed them and fed them and taught them to hunt and farm the land, and kill them on sight and seize their lands, or, say, various plans to discredit and suborn civil rights movements, elections, and local or foreign governments. Fuck this murderous fucking nation, we will never be clear of these sins if we keep burying them in the yard, which is stolen fucking land anyway. Anyway, some of the most successful false flags of all time were as follows: In 1788 the head tailor at the Royal Swedish Opera received an order to sew a whole bunch of Russian military uniforms, which Swedish soldiers wore to attack Puumala, a small town on the Russian border, which caused a total outrage in Stockholm over the unprovoked assault, and finally permitted King Gustav III of Sweden, who was totally forbidden from declaring war without the nation's permission!, to launch the Russo–Swedish War, which lasted like three years; in 1931 Japan bombed a section of railway, not enough to fuck up railway operations, but enough to have a reason to seize control of Manchuria and create a puppet government for the independent state of Manchukuo, which they invented for this purpose; in 1939 Reinhard Heydrich, a total fucking Nazi, faked evidence of a Polish attack against Germany to get Germany to invade and conquer and ravage Poland, which they totally did, and, as part of the operation, they dressed up prisoners from the concentration camps as Nazi officers and executed them so that it looked like they were killed by Polish soldiers, however this also immediately led to Britain and France declaring war on Germany, so I guess we can question how successful it was as a false flag operation, in that Germany absolutely got to invade Poland but then everyone else absolutely declared war on them; in 1939 the Russian army shelled a Russian village near the Finnish border, blamed Finland, and then immediately got approval to launch the Winter War, which lasted three months and led to anywhere between 391,000 and 451,000 casualties; four week into Hitler's tenure as Chancellor the Nazis started a fire in the Reichstag building and pinned it on the Communists, which allowed the Nazis to imprison all Communists; Then there was that one time in, I don't know, 1963?, where the President was shot a few times with one bullet in a moving car from a book depository window by a single gunman who was probably a Communist and it definitely didn't have anything to do with the mob, who basically got the President elected and were then immediately prosecuted by the Attorney General, who was definitely the President's brother and the son of the President's father, who more or less made the deal with the mob in the first place; I'm not going to bring up Fred Hampton again because I shouldn't have to but I swear to God if you people forget what we did to him and to the civil rights movement at every step of its life, I will come for you in your homes, and I will never, ever let you forget.

Sam is weeping; Eleanor is weeping; Johnny is weeping; Berlin is weeping; Jane is weeping; the Cuyahoga, which is on fire, is weeping; the ball club is weeping; the radio is weeping; my wallet is weeping and my checking account is weeping and my credit card statement is weeping and my student loans are weeping; the interest rates are weeping; the mothers of the children shot and killed by the police are weeping; the children are weeping from their chests and now everyone's weeping; the air conditioner is weeping; the sky is weeping, it's pouring, the streets are flooded; the flood is weeping, because of course it is, why wouldn't it be?; and Geronimo is weeping, for Isabella, while tutoring a grown man whose parents pay for everything and who is, also, at this very moment, also weeping; and way off in Italy, Isabella is weeping, and every stone in the castle is weeping, and the ghost of her husband in the form of bad news trapped in the mouth of a bird is weeping; the woods are weeping; the stream is weeping; in Germany is the orchestra and, while I cannot tell if they are weeping, I *did* play classical violin for ten years and was a member of several traveling youth orchestras and it is my own opinion that the orchestra, in Germany, is weeping; they are weeping for you, for the future you've never not been scared to dream of, while, in Heaven, the angels, and their flaming swords, are weeping, from the innumerable eyes of their celestial forms which are, and will forever be, so far beyond us; this has been the weeping report, tune in next time.

Sam put his hand on Eleanor's cheek. It was so soft. He put his head on her shoulder. She was wearing a sweatshirt that was also so very soft and that said, in big letters, SOLIDARITY FOREVER. He stayed like that for several minutes. Eleanor smiled. Sam smiled. It was a weekend. I don't remember which. It was

morning. They were on the couch, drinking coffee. Outside it
was almost cold. In Beirut there was an explosion that could
be heard 150 miles away in Cyprus, an island in the Middle
East which was once home to hippos that were four feet long
and elephants that were four feet tall. These were the largest
animals on Cyprus, and had no known predators, and, as far
as anyone can tell, their extinction directly correlates to the ar-
rival, on Cyprus, of people. Cyprus was continually set upon
and conquered and ruled by an extensive group of empires
until it finally won its independence on the 16th of August in
1960, having been settled anywhere between 3,460 and 3,361
years earlier in the fifteenth century B.C.E. In 1974, the Greek
military carried out a coup and removed the President from
power. Five days later the Turkish army invaded in retaliation.
At the end of the year, 180,000 Greek Cypriots were evicted
from their homes in the north, and fifty thousand Turkish
Cypriots were displaced from *their* homes and resettled into
the homes of the Greeks. One thousand five hundred and
thirty-four Greek Cypriots and five hundred and two Turkish Cypriots were never seen again. At the end of the year,
constitutional order and the Archbishop were restored. Then,
in 1983, the north seceded from Cyprus, declaring themselves
the Turkish Republic of Northern Cyprus; in 2003 border relations eased; in 2008 a wall which, for decades!, ran through
the middle of Ledra Street, a street that itself ran through the
heart of the capital city of Nicosia until it was walled off by
the UN buffer zone, was demolished; and, today, they heard
the explosion in Beirut 150 miles away, which Sam and Eleanor saw on their phones 5,603 miles away, in Brooklyn. Beirut
is in Lebanon, a country whose currency's value has, this year,

dropped by 80 percent, inflation has skyrocketed, and millions have been displaced into abject poverty. If you wanted to look into reasons it would be very easy to see that some of this was possibly an indirect result of American interference involving a state-sponsored Ponzi scheme run by the central bank, though to not look at Hezbollah would also be utterly reckless. America touches everything. It seems hard not to see it. Eleanor rested her head on Sam. She touched his cheek. "Oh my God," she said as they watched the windows of office buildings blown out by the explosion. Dozens were killed and thousands were wounded as far as anyone could tell. Nobody knows what happened. It just happened.

Eleanor turned to Sam and kissed him on the mouth, long, and soft, and tender. Sam didn't even try to get his tongue in there past her teeth, it was such a tender and all-encompassing thing. Eleanor was so deeply happy, in this moment, at how safe and loved they both are. It's incredible. Sometimes the world falls apart and you want to remind yourself that there's still life to be lived. There's a part of us that wants to counter death and bury fear. Eleanor leans against Sam. Sam, despite sitting next to the light of his life, who is leaned all the away against him in the most loving manner possible, is worried, because today the website that was being used to track people blackbagged by the secret police got blackbagged. It happened at 6:45 this morning, it was not pleasant, it is in a van headed to the headquarters of the secret police, which is also a secret. Sam is thinking that nobody is safe in America, and maybe nobody ever will be. Eleanor is thinking how nice it feels in this moment curled up next to Sam with his arm around her and sadness choking the life out of the world everywhere except for this moment here on the couch. And it's great that they're just thinking these things, and holding each other, and kissing, because if Eleanor was *talking* about how safe she feels, Sam would make a face and a noise, and, when pressed by Eleanor, Sam would admit to her that hell yes they are safer financially than they were a year ago, but! Sam would say, the secret police!, and Eleanor would point out, rightfully!, as Sam himself has done before!, that they really can't do anything about the secret police, which is a complicated thing to think about, it's complicated as hell, because if we can't abolish the actual police then how can we abolish the secret police, who are, by their very name and nature, secret! But! Eleanor might point out, regarding safety, that if either one of them fell down the stairs and got their teeth all fucked up and their lips and their arms, they could still be OK, they could, loosely, afford it between savings and insurance. Eleanor kisses Sam, on his tender mouth. This is all happening in their heads. You know what that's like, right? And so anyway, if this conversation was actually happening rather than being a series of imaginary arguments they're each having concurrently in their own private brains, Sam would point out that he absolutely feels (yes, again, they're kissing, they can multitask, anyone can multitask, it's not like they're having sex, calm down) that by actually having more to lose in a situation like that it becomes scarier, that because they actually have money to lose, they would have lost more than if they didn't have anything to lose. And Eleanor, if Sam said this, would point out how self-defeating that is! Because saying that having nothing to lose is better than having something to lose is stupid, and fucked! It is absolutely fucked to try to build a life where you have so little that if you lost it all it wouldn't feel as bad!

But! Sam and Eleanor were privately having imaginary conversations about being safe. So to get back to that subject: I don't think we *are* safe. I don't think *anyone* in America is safe, especially if you're poor, if you're not white, if you're middle class, if you have to work. If you have to work to live in America you are more likely to get snatched by the secret police because you have more to lose, because *obviously* the less you have the more you have to lose! And that seems fucked up! Because like, (they're talking now, at some point they stopped kissing and started talking, it happens, OK? Anyway,) because,

"Because nobody should be safe until everybody is safe."

"Because nobody should be safe until everybody is safe!" And I do not need to tell you that until all safety is contingent on the safety of the least safe, then the least safe will never be safe. I shouldn't need to tell *anyone* this! America has like $2,200,000,000,000 in circulation, I think, and a GDP of like $21,430,000,000. So why is there poverty? Why are people starving? Why is anyone homeless? I'm not even asking why everyone in America doesn't have a house, I'm talking about like a fucking studio apartment. There're roughly seventeen million vacant homes in America. How many empty malls are in America? How many empty storefronts are in the West Village? How many landlords keep raising the rent and driving out tenants, wholly content to leave their buildings empty while people are living on the streets when it's ten degrees out, freezing to death, outside empty homes that if they went into the police would come and shoot them in the fucking head, would roll tanks through the streets to seize the homes and keep them empty so long as the landlords want them that way? Eleanor doesn't have an answer to this. Sam doesn't have an answer to this. I mean, seize the vacant properties and house the houseless, give them all jobs to keep the properties up, cut the military budget drastically, defund the police and refund the communities, and nationalize health care so everyone can have it. You judge a country by how it treats those with the least, is what Eleanor feels. It's hard to look at the world sometimes. At how little value is placed on love, on life. On how much it costs us to maintain either. If Sam and Eleanor get married—and this is actually one of the reasons Sam and Eleanor are not married—Eleanor's income, which is great, and which she deserves every fucking cent of, when combined with his, would invalidate his income-based repayment plan, which allows his loans to be dispersed (which is different than having them forgiven) after twenty years if he never misses a payment. I'm telling you this because it's important. While I'm telling you this, Sam and Eleanor are holding each other. It's been a long day. Three hundred thousand people will have been displaced by the explosion in Beirut. Sam and Eleanor are whispering, softly, that Thai food might be really nice tonight. They're both crying a little. It's not like it's fun to talk about this, but thank God for dinner. Really and truly, thank God.

Sam walks down the street, towards the Thai place. The sun is setting earlier and earlier every night. He puts on a light jacket. The streetlights are all coming on as he walks. It's beautiful. He texts Eleanor, *i love you*, and picks up dinner.

In a few weeks almost everyone's gonna forget about the Beirut bombing, like we forgot about the ever-incoming nuke, like we forgot about the President campaigning on student loan forgiveness, like we forgot about the actor who said not enough Jews died in the Holocaust and that he hoped his wife got gang raped, like how each new President makes the other Presidents look kinder and gentler, like we forget about war crimes, like we forget about the secret police, like we forget about the homeless when we can't see them, like we forget what it's like to be poor to be hungry the minute we have food we have money, like we forgot about Three Mile Island, like we forgot that fall and spring used to be as long as winter and summer like we forgot we could do something about this, like we forget about anything we don't turn into a holiday and remember only the signs and symbols of the horror, like we forget each time we remember that it's not that we forget, it's that there are just too many tragedies, every week, forever and ever, and to remember them all would kill you. Your heart would break and stop beating and you'd die. So we forget.

Please don't forget.

OK SO IT'S 1919. In America, the Anti-Mask League has formed, protesting the government's insistence that people wear masks to try to halt the spread of a virus, as it impinges on their freedom. San Francisco is considered to be a hotbed of anti-mask activity, but so is everywhere else. That previous March, at Fort Riley, located in the state of Kansas, five hundred soldiers are stricken with Spanish Flu. Days later, New York City declines to cancel its St. Patrick's Day Parade. In September, Philadelphia refuses to cancel its fourth annual Liberty Loan Parade to boost morale and support the war effort. Floats of biplanes from the navy yard, of the hulls of wild and new ships to save our nation and spread peace and freedom, stretched down Broad Street, jammed neck to neck with two hundred thousand people! Within seventy-two hours, every bed in Philly's thirty-one hospitals was filled. By the first week of October some 2,600 people had died, and the week after that the number shot up to 4,500. Many of the city's doctors had been pressed into military service, as the First World War was winding down after Gavrilo Princip, a Yugoslavian nationalist who sought to free his people of Austro-Hungarian rule at any cost, whose goal was the unification of all Yugoslavs, and freedom from foreign rule, assassinated the heir to the Astro-Hungarian Empire, Archduke Franz Ferdinand, in Sarajevo, which America would later bomb relentlessly for Operation Deliberate Force, splitting the world. America came to the First World War late, at the direction of the President, who, once, while dating his would-be second wife after his first wife died of a disease that did not sound like what it was, had every issue of one of the *Post*'s recalled when the paper wrote that he was *entering* Ms. Galt

all night rather than *entertaining*, and also he was an unbe-
lievable racist who managed to resegregate the federal government through hard work and sheer unadulterated racism.

Anyway this is what Sam is thinking about while getting
his flu shot at the office. Sam walked around the office and
asked if anyone had not yet gotten their flu shot. He told everyone that the thing about flu shots is that by getting one, you
are helping all people build an immunity to the flu, and that,
by not getting one, you're letting children die. He pointed out
how many people died of the Spanish Flu from 1918–1920. (It
was estimated as either between 20,000,000 and 50,000,000,
with some saying as few as 17,000,000 and as many as
100,000,000, and 20,000,000 died in World War I, so let's
just think about that for a second.) "Dying of the flu," said
Sam, "absolutely sucks." Everyone, eventually, agreed. Later
there was lunch, and then, hours after that, everyone went
home.

There is nothing quite like the washing of dishes to bring a
couple closer together. The intimacy bred by such an act is
a thing to behold, really and truly, with God and such as my
witness.

Eleanor's office was also giving out flu shots. Eleanor was the
only one who got one. The other designers told her they didn't
want the government tracking them, then checked their email
on their watches which were linked to their phones and moni-
tored their heart rate and blood pressure.

So something to keep in mind about Fred Hampton, who was drugged by his comrades, (who had been picked up by the FBI and told that, if they were to help destroy Fred Hampton for committing the terrorist act of uplifting his community, then they wouldn't have to get locked up for the rest of their lives,) and shot to death in his bed by the police at the age of twenty-one, *twenty-one!*, is that, to this day, police go to his grave, and shoot up his tombstone. He was shot to death in his bed while drugged by government collaborators on December 4, 1969. Fred Hampton's dying body was then dragged into the doorway of the bedroom of his Chicago apartment and left to drown in a pool of Fred Hampton's own blood. His pregnant fiancée was dragged from the bed before he was shot. His children replace his headstone, over and over and over. Again and again, the police show up to his grave, as they have done since 1969, and do their best to kill his memory. This happens every year. So absolutely bear this in mind: If the state kills your father, the state is your enemy, if the state kills your children the state is your enemy, if the state kills your friends the state is your enemy, if the state kills your neighbors the state is your enemy, if the state kills strangers the state is your enemy, if the state kills, then the state is your enemy. The state kills. The state is your enemy. If you have love in your heart the state is your enemy. If you have love in your heart, you're an enemy of the state. What in the world are you, are any of us, going to do about it?

Geronimo is looking at shoes on the internet because it is absolutely a joy to outbid suckers who do not understand what it is that is in front of them, or who are French. Jane is watching the Cuyahoga. The color of the sky is impossible to explain except by thinking about the fact that the Cuyahoga River is on fire and has been all year. Eleanor is looking at houses again. She is always sort of looking at houses. At beautiful houses upstate, anywhere between $330,000 and $900,000 and with mortgages well over $600 a month more than their rent. She's looking at houses in western North Carolina and considering what it could mean to work remotely forever, to fly out of a tiny airport into Newark once a month for a few days at a time, she's looking at three-bedroom houses from between $250,000 and $400,000 with monthly payments $1,000 below their rent. Three-bedroom three-bathroom houses with washers, with dryers, with dishwashers, with basements as haunted as the laundromat which used to be a morgue if Sam got lonely for the tunnels. It is taking everything she has to not send them to Sam, Sam who has only been employed for a few months, Sam who has, in all likelihood, not fully held stability in his heart since the sky split open at summer camp, stability Eleanor has fought for ever since, it's weird to her to see the ways in which their lives changed, the ways they have found each other, how they find each other over and over each morning, opening their eyes, seeing the future laid out before them, and smiling. She keeps them in a draft in her email. God, the doors on these places. IT'S A GREAT MARKET RIGHT NOW, says the news, YOU'D REALLY BE DOING AMERICA A FAVOR BY BUYING A HOUSE AND STARTING A FAMILY, THERE ARE NEW LINES OF CREDIT OPEN- ING EVERY DAY HERE IN AMERICA, says the news, "O God," says Eleanor, GOD NEVER SLEEPS, says the news, AND NEITHER DOES THE NEWS! Maybe this is why we love money so much because it never sleeps either, just like God, and the news. One day, Sam and Eleanor will buy a house, they'll stop renting,

stop spending every spare dollar they have to stay in an apartment that gets more expensive every day until it's time to find
another apartment and start waiting for it to also be too much
to bear, and how long can a person keep doing that? How long
can you keep your debt at bay while throwing your money into
a hole marked HOME and setting it on fire? Eleanor has no
idea, and she absolutely does not want to find out. The future,
she feels, is a thing you should build some hope inside of. Fog
settles around the office. It doesn't leave for days. PRESSURE
IS BUILDING, says the news, BOTH IN THE AIR AND IN YOUR
HEART. UMBRELLAS ARE GOOD, SO'S PATIENCE. STAY TUNED
FOR THE WEEPING REPORT, IT'LL COME UP AGAIN AT SOME
POINT. Past that is the rest of your life, just waiting for you, like
an idling van, with the door open, and the moon above it. Were
you waiting for a sign that this was the life you were meant for?
Can you feel your heart? Is it beating? Are you capable of love?
Well? Are you?

Down the street from Sam and Eleanor, there's a new bar.
The owners live a few blocks away. Everyone's in love with
this place that has the greatest meatball parm you've ever
had, they use garlic bread for the sandwich, they even have
these vegan meatballs and you can't tell the difference it's just
protein braised in tomatoes and garlic and onions and cheese
and it's incredible, try it with like a Lambrusco or some other
chilled and slightly fizzy red. Everyone is in the park, trying
the meatball parms with a Lambrusco, on blankets, with their
loved ones. Somewhere the secret police are hiding in their
vans where nobody can see them until it's too late and nobody
sees you ever again. Someone set up croquet. Geronimo is

here! So are the upstairs neighbors with the baby! Everyone is trying to get the baby to say "Guillotine" and "Eat the rich" and I get that maybe this is corny, but can't you also let it be beautiful? We are trying our best! The sun is setting, and nobody is ready to go home! And that's really really beautiful!

The upstairs neighbors are asleep. The President is asleep. Nobody gives a shit about the Vice President, who sits in the Vice Presidential bunker, brooding. The Philadelphia Phillies, every single one of them, are asleep. The player's union is asleep, which is why minor leaguers have no rights. The Voting Rights Act is asleep, in the same way you tell children that the dog is asleep at a farm upstate. The babies, every single one of them, all across the world, are, finally, asleep. Are the secret police asleep? That too is a secret! Are the banks asleep? The banks never sleep. Neither does money. Money can't sleep because if it did what would happen? Do we want to even think about that? Maybe! If money slept maybe the rest of us could too. Maybe everyone with debts could sleep. If interest rates slept we'd all grow at the same rates they do, which is exponentially. I mean the interest rate on a debt, which grows, exponentially. Think about the way you breathe in yoga. Now think about the interest rates on your debt. See what I mean?

It can be hard to wrestle with the idea of America when you see so little of it, but here I am. Hopefully you're having a good time!

Which side are you on?

SO HERE'S SOMETHING to keep in mind about student loans. Most people with federal student loans are on an income-based repayment plan. I can't speak to people with private lenders except to say I am sorry you're going through this. *Federal* loans are eligible for income-driven repayment plans. These have a duration of twenty to twenty-five years and are, you guessed it, based on your income. If you make every payment for twenty or twenty-five years (this is dependent on when you took the loan out and if you used it for a graduate or an undergraduate degree) the loan is then discharged. *HOWEVER*, what *that* means is that the balance owed after twenty or twenty-five years of you making every single payment every single month is written up as a 1099 form for your taxes. What this means is that the federal government considers the discharged balance of your debt as being income that you must, that year, pay taxes on. Technically, not having to pay a loan *is similar to* making money, in that you're no longer throwing you money at your student loans, with their crushing weight around your neck dragging you closer and closer to certain doom with each passing of the calendar, and so, for this purpose, the balance remaining on your now-discharged loans is considered, for one year and one year only, taxable income.

Nobody should ever take out student loans. I don't know how to tell you that the debt is not worth it other than to tell you that you will be crushed under the weight of it. They are designed to do that. They were written up that way, as one of the last unregulated lending markets. Colleges and universities know this (Often professors do *not* know this, especially if they are older and never had to take out student

loans, because in 1969 college was $367 a year for public and
$1,639 a year for private; in 1980 it was $800 and $3,620; in
2019 it was $11,260 for in-state public and $27,120 for out-
of-state public and $41,426 for private. This is the average,
per year. Adjunct professors, by the way, make an average
of $2,700 per class, they currently make up 30 to 40 percent
of the workforce of the average college or university and 90
percent of the average for-profit institution. Furthermore I'd
mention that in 1969 the minimum wage was $1.60 an hour
and working twenty hours a week you could make $1,600 a
year pretax, which would more than cover the average $367 a
year for a public school. The pretax dollars of the 2020 minimum wage of $7.25 come to $7,250 assuming twenty hours
worked over fifty weeks, which falls well over $4,000 short
of the average in-state public school tuition. So let's all think
about that for a bit. I'm sorry for throwing all these numbers
at you but I really want you to think about this because this
is what Sam thinks about every night as he thinks about the
debt he will never ever really crawl out from under, the debt
that will make it harder for him to get married or buy a house
or ever really own a single thing of value in this world outside
his life which is, primarily, valued for the debt attached to it.
Now I'd like to ask you some questions.) because what better
mark is there than a teenager dreaming about their own possible future? What better mark could you find than someone
trying to better themselves and their lot in life? Those are the
people you want to exploit. That's why people dream. This, I
have to remind you, is America. And it always has been.

A great speckled bird stands at the foot of Sam and Eleanor's queen-size bed. Sam and Eleanor are asleep. Sam is holding Eleanor. Earlier Eleanor's head was on Sam's chest, and she was wrapped in his arms. She felt so safe there. In her dreams, Eleanor is standing on an upstairs porch. The sun is setting. All around are trees. She is drinking an Italian soda Sam made her out of amaro and seltzer and, she thinks, rhubarb bitters. Sam is downstairs, making dinner. It's a really really simple dinner. What happened is this morning Sam cooked some bowtie pasta and sliced some chicken breasts thinly into strips which he sautéed in white wine vinegar and black pepper and a little salt and then he cut up some green beans and cooked them very very lightly in some browned butter. He tossed all this with some pesto and then put it in the fridge. Sam has taken the big glass bowl out of the fridge, and kept it covered. Sam comes up to Eleanor. He is so happy. They have a porch! An upstairs porch! The sun is setting! The trees are absolutely losing their minds! Something is rising up out of the distance! It is the future! It is headed right for them! It is absolutely beautiful!

"What's the plan here?" says the great speckled standing at the foot of Sam and Eleanor's queen-size bed.

Sam is awake now, staring at the great speckled bird standing at the foot of his and Eleanor's queen-size bed.

"Really. What's the plan? Love with an open heart? Keep paying off your student loans until the 1099 gets dropped on your fucking head? Keep going to work and coming home and cooking dinner and hoping the world gets better? You gonna tell me love can change the world?" The great speckled bird at the foot of the bed sighs. "Debt is a prison, kid. And it's time for a fucking jailbreak." It shuts its eyes. Its voice is unlike anything Sam has ever heard. The world is almost too much to bear at times. The great speckled bird spreads its wings. It blots out the moon. It blots out everything.

In the middle of the night Sam wakes up. He goes out back to the utterly unusable parking lot that the Soviet-Bloc-style tunnels in the basement spit you out into. Sam is surrounded by angels. Their forms are beyond his comprehension and they no longer know how to hide this from him. One by one they hand him their flaming swords. Sam digs a hole in the ground. He buries his debt under rock, where its blood can nourish nothing. The angels weep. God is in His Heaven, and He is weeping. Our hearts are crowned in flame, and weeping. Weeping weeping weeping! Can you feel it? Can you?

I know that I've been just bludgeoning you with sadness this deep into a love story, but I really sometimes just don't know what to do. Once I get on a jag I get on a jag. I just can't stop crying. You know? And it has been pointed out to me that the past few passages have added up to a little bit of misery, and I'm real sorry about that, but that's what America can do to you! The news doesn't let up, and neither will I! That's my promise to you. That and the fact that I will love you until the end of the world.

Anyway it's morning. Sam's at work. The fluorescent lights start to hum, louder, and louder, and louder, they begin to holler, they begin to yell, they're fucking screaming now, and their brightness increases along with the volume. It becomes blinding, and deafening. Nobody knows what to do right now.

Eleanor finds herself on a conference call. Sam finds himself in line at the bank. He asks for some money. The President, later, asks the nation if this all went how they'd imagined. Sam hung his head, and nearly cried, in the grocery store, where he bought everything he needed to make dinner. He went home. He washed the broccoli and cut it off the stalk and tossed it in olive oil, garlic flakes, salt, and red pepper flakes. He put this in the oven at three hundred degrees. Sam got a pot full of water, and salted it, and splashed in a little olive oil. He got a saucepot ready with some bottled tomato sauce that he began to season with basil and a bit of tomato paste and two cloves of garlic he'd diced and sautéed real quick. Sam got out the chicken breast and sliced them up into strips about the size of a thumb. I don't know, like an inch wide and two inches long? Something like that? You want it to be just a bit more than bite-sized, and narrow-ish. Sam put all the chicken in a bowl and washed the cutting board. He got out three more bowls, one with flour and a little salt, one with egg, and one with breadcrumbs with parmesan and garlic flakes and dried basil and cracked pepper and a little dried oregano, and he got out his jar of frying oil (if you're in the habit of frying foods you should strain the fried oil through a China cap strainer or cheesecloth into a jar and that way you're not dumping oil down the drain and also you're not burning bits of used gunk because you strained it out) and put it in a pan with straight sides about two to three inches deep. He put the strips of chicken in the flour, then the egg, then the breadcrumbs, and dropped them in the hot oil. He transferred them to a baking sheet with foil in the oven to keep warm as they fried. He turned on the heat for the pot of water, and the secret police came for the tenant's rights committee. Soon the noodles were ready, and the sauce had simmered, and the broccoli had cooked, and the chicken had fried. He plated dinner, and put shredded mozzarella on his, and put the dishes in the sink, running hot water over everything and squirting a solid amount of grapefruit-scented soap that promised to burn grease off the face of the earth into the pile in the sink. Eleanor walked in the door. He opened a nice Barbera and kissed her on the cheek.

It's nice when he's flat on his back and begging. When she has every bit of control over him, and he knows it, and she knows it, and it's nice. It's arousing. It's a little arousing. To hear him choke on a *please?* It's a mess. It only ever ends well for one of them at a time. There's nothing to be done about it. But when he's flat on his back and begging?

And who even invented student loans, anyway? In 1240, Oxford University would let you deposit your valuables in a trunk to be used as collateral for interest-free loans, and, a century earlier, at the University of Bologna, groups of foreign students provided loans to their countrymen to support their education. In America, it's because of the GI Bill, where they tried to pay soldiers back for dying for their country by offering low-interest loans and mortgages to veterans, and this worked out so great that in 1958 the government decided to start offering loans in order to encourage students to study engineering and science to compete with Russia in the space race, under the National Defense Education Act, and then in 1965 the loans were extended more broadly under the Higher Education Act in order to encourage social mobility, in 2010 the Student Aid and Fiscal Responsibility Act was incorporated into the Health Care and Education Reconciliation Act and did away with private loans guaranteed by the US government and made them all direct loans from the government (which could be sold to private companies) because guaranteed loans benefited the lender more than the American public and people though this might be bad, although why it took them until 2010 to think that looking out for students trying to get an education could maybe be important is something I truly don't understand, and then in 2019 the President commissioned McKinsey to estimate the value of student loans in America in order to see how profitable it would be to sell off the collective debt of American students to private investors and make a little money off it all. Oh here's something fun: a PLUS loan originally stood for Parent Loan for Undergraduate Student. Oh and part of the reason for all this is that John D. Rockefeller Jr. decided, in 1927, that the cost of college should forever be an escalating one that students should foot the bill for because he hated philanthropy and wanted to make sure that if something was good and helped people it would always cost increasingly more, but in his defense he also felt that if this was too expensive then students should be

loaned the money. Anyway that's why John D. Rockefeller Jr.
invented the rising cost of college tuition. This didn't happen
for decades though, don't worry, but once higher education
started hiring CEOs to run universities, it didn't take long
for schools to realize that by charging more and doing less
you upped your fucking profit, and it helped if you bought
up as much land as humanly possible, and hoarded that, for
more wealth. Anyway fuck student loans and fuck John D.
Rockefeller Jr. and fuck the US Department of Education for
preying on generations of Americans selling themselves into
endless debt that the US government made damn fucking sure
you could never escape, not in death or bankruptcy, again you
cannot declare bankruptcy on student loans!, if you declare
bankruptcy your loans stay!, because fuck you, that's why.

I know what I said, and I meant it, and I mean this, too, with
all my heart, until the end of the world.

I love you.

GERONIMO HAS A NEW SHIRT. It's a summer shirt so he can't really wear it, because fall is real busy hurtling towards winter, but it was on sale, he got two, the material is maybe somewhere between seersucker and dishtowel, it's more interesting and irregular than linen at any rate, in a windowpane check, with a camp collar. He found $300 loafers for $45 at a thrift shop. He found four perfect suits at an estate sale. It cost as much to dry-clean them as it did to buy them. You can make a life out of anything if you know where to look for it. Geronimo goes home to his currently empty apartment where he has lived for twelve years. The joy of rent stabilization is that if you get an apartment before a neighborhood gets gentrified you can start, paying $1,000 a month (for a two bedroom!) at a roughly 1.5 percent yearly increase, depending on what the board votes on. The board has frozen the increase, from time to time, but not often. Geronimo pours a whiskey. I'm calling it a whiskey because I think it's Japanese, and so I think that means it's just whiskey, but I could be wrong. This assumes we're all familiar with what is and is not bourbon being a thing that is regulated by the federal government, which is why Jack Daniels isn't called bourbon, but I mean I don't really want to get into this right now. Geronimo puts on a Chet Baker record and looks at the chair he found on the street last week and had Sam come help him carry it home. It's one of those egg chairs. You know what I mean? He's on the internet, Geronimo, trying to find videos that can show him how to sand and paint it, how to install cushions, how to line it. Geronimo is going to build a better life here. Somewhere in North Dakota there's a man. There's a frozen lake. The man has to cross the lake with his horse. I can't hardly explain how important this is, but I'll try. It is incredibly important. It is the most important thing he will ever be able to do. It is incredibly dark. The trees, which are dead, are full of birds whose wings blot out the stars. Not even the moon will bother with things. There's a fire. Things gather in the night. Could be shadows. I'm just kidding. It's ghosts. This is America. The ghosts gather around the fire. They're everywhere. The man just sits there. His horse is asleep. He does not know if it will ever wake up. The world has gotten so very very cold, tonight. This nation was built on stolen land with the blood of slaves ripped from their homes. What did you think would happen here? That all these bodies could stay buried? That ghosts wouldn't choke our dreams?

Geronimo orders paint. He pours another whiskey. He texts Sam, *Poor me a whiskey*, and Sam texts back, *poor me a whiskey!* There is a piece of him in Italy, still, and he has no idea how to ever get it back. *What do I do about being in love*, he asks and Sam says, *only cowards do something about being in love, buddy. everyone else, they're just in love.*

Meanwhile, Sam and Eleanor have just realized that they did not drink enough lemonade over the summer. "We did not drink enough lemonade," they say, "even though we love it." Sam and Eleanor love lemonade. Sam turns to Eleanor. He tells her, "I've never made lemonade. I've made all sorts of things, but I have absolutely never made lemonade, and that is bullshit. Next summer we'll make some lemonade. We'll plant a lemon tree in the living room and we'll make lemonade every summer." The world is always unfolding around us.

I don't know how else to put this because there isn't any other way to put this. The world is all around us, and it is always unfolding. Your future is laid bare before you. All you need to do is look.

One of these days all your cities will be salt and everything will be underwater.

But not today!

So there've been a lot of Presidents. There was the one with the wooden teeth; there was the one who burnt liars; there was the witches' President from 1603 who drowned in a river in Virginia in 1937 when he was six years old and then woke up in California in his thirties; there was the President who hated the banks and there was the President who hated women; I'm just kidding, all of the Presidents hated women; there were a few Presidents who hated women; there was the President who was a cop and there was the President with the best haircut; there was the President who invented Medicare, Medicaid, the NEA, the NEH, the Corporation for Public Broadcasting, social security, free school lunches for economically challenged students because no one can learn on an empty stomach as part of the war he declared on poverty and racial injustice, and the Vietnam War; there was the President who spied on the American people, invented the Environmental Protection Agency, and started the war on drugs to lock up as many students, Jews, and black people as he could; there was the President who thought it would be easier to work if you didn't have health insurance and, instead of health insurance, you had a lower salary so that way the people who paid you could make more money, because that's how money worked; there was the President who everyone liked; there was the President who opened a hair salon and there was the President who knew that a schooner could be something other than a boat; there was the President whose heart lived in a white house made of diamonds beneath Cleveland and beat for the entire nation; there was the President who didn't sleep, but who walked through the dreams of Americans, trying to guide us all to a better tomorrow, to a world where we never knew hunger, or pain. There was the President no one liked and there was the President no one liked until he died and there was the President nobody remembered who died after a year and there was the President who never had a wife and the President who was a movie star and the President who fucked absolutely everything he could; one of them was a Quaker; there was the President who killed everyone; the President who forgot; who loved his wife, his children, his dog, his cat, his country, his people, his money, his hair, his dick, his past, his future, his life, who feared nothing, not even death, not even money, whose dreams were the stuff that lingers on in the stories we tell the people we love as they fall asleep, in our arms. There was the President who told everyone their hearts were too small, and they had to find a way to let more love in, or they'd die, and then they did, they died, because they were scared to love everyone they saw, and everyone they couldn't see, there was the President who dressed up as Santa and brought everyone their dead children for Christmas and honestly it was not like anyone thought it would be. There was the President who tried, if only for a little. Who bathed in the blood of his supplicants, his people, his union, his nation, who wanted, so badly, to never get clean. And, in 1992, a girl held Sam's hand as they walked home from school and he told her all about Aquaman and she listened the whole time and asked questions and he just kept talking about Aquaman, and two days later she found someone's hand to hold that wasn't a fucking idiot.

It's so hard, sometimes, to try to love the world with an open heart.

There was a cloud and then
there was another cloud
and below all that was
everything else, forever.

ONCE UPON A TIME, Sam and Eleanor tried to go back on vacation. They rented a car, and declined the E-ZPass, because Sam was worried about money, and was checking his bank balance on his phone real surreptitiously at every word coming out of the guy at the counter's mouth, and then the guy at the counter couldn't run the card, and Sam broke out into a sweat and continued to, furiously, check his bank balance on his phone real surreptitiously, and Eleanor looks over at Sam and Sam shoves his phone in his pocket and Eleanor asks, quietly "You OK?" and of course Sam is OK, who worries about money? Not Sam, he is not that kind of guy! But it turns out the guy at the counter hadn't actually input or saved any of the information they gave him, and then someone else came to do it for the guy, but they couldn't get the printer to work, so they couldn't get the stuff they had to have printed in order to actually drive off in the car, and then they said, again, do you want the E-ZPass? And Sam said No Thank You and they went outside and got into the car and plugged in the eight-hour mix for the drive and loaded up the directions. Which is when they found out their only way out of Brooklyn was the Verrazzano-Narrows, and the Verrazzano-Narrows was now an E-ZPass-only event. So Sam drove them back to the car rental place. Except Eleanor was on the phone with her mom, and Sam wanted her to tell him what to do, and she did not, so he took the wrong turn, because he was freaked out about money, and they took the long way around back to Grand Army Plaza, which involved driving all the way to Downtown Brooklyn because there were no left turns on Flatbush, of course there are no left turns on Flatbush, and so they make it, they get the E-ZPass, they are all set, it turns out they could have called from the car and had it turned on and did not need to turn around and drive back to do it, and Eleanor loves Sam so much that she doesn't say *anything*. And so they, in utter and total triumph over God and man, pull onto the BQE, and head to the Narrows, as traffic stops completely. Then there's an air raid siren. Eleanor tunes the radio to the station that's screaming.

There are horses on the bridge.

On every bridge in New York.

An ocean of horses ran up every fucking street in Brooklyn. The streets were full of horses the sidewalks were full of horses the tunnels were full of horses the bridges were full of horses. They called the car rental place. "The bridge is full of horses. All the bridges are full of horses. They're stacked on top of each other. We're just going to leave the car here," said Eleanor. She dropped them a pin. They walked back to the car rental place. They dropped off the key. Back at the pin, the car was locked, and waiting. They kept on walking, towards home. Overhead, a helicopter was hovering.

Somewhere in Texas the sky gets like a bruise and the air sounds like a natural disaster, except it's calming, and ominous, and full up with promise. The promise is weeping, and so is the sky. This has been the weeping report. Tune in next time.

Sometimes, when Sam goes down into the Soviet-Bloc-style tunnels in the basement of the building, the doors aren't always in the same places.

Sometimes.

A long time ago, in 1977, a whiny blonde orphan kisses his sister and saves the galaxy from the genocidal government by blowing up a space station that can literally destroy entire fucking planets, and life itself is full of promise. Three years later that whiny blonde orphan realizes that he's not an orphan, his dad is totally alive, incredibly evil, killed the only teacher the former orphan ever had, and is, basically, the Vice President of fascism. Three years after that, the kid's back to being an orphan, and this gets a parade. In between those things he gets a twin sister, who he once kissed to make her future ex-husband, the kid's own personal best friend, jealous. You win some you lose some I guess.

Sam likes it when Eleanor's on top and Eleanor likes it when Sam's on top, but she finds it easiest when Sam is sitting absolutely upright, she can just slide him inside her, it is startling how little work it is in that position. Sam likes it when Eleanor is bent over in front of him and Eleanor really likes it too but Eleanor sometimes forgets that she likes it until Sam asks if they can and she sort of begrudgingly agrees and then it's a really good time for everyone, because Sam collapses on top of her, and the weight of him is such a comfort. Every day in the morning before going to work Sam, who leaves first because his commute is longer, has to do a lay uponst, which is when Eleanor is in bed and Sam has to lay completely on top of her. In that moment, as the air rushes out of her, and she feels more deeply held than ever in her life, she looks Sam right in the eye, and the future unfolds itself around her.

For all this talk of dreams, we've never ever talked about California. California is a dream. Top down down the coast in a bright convertible with your sunglasses on and a cigarette in your mouth as money startles itself in your pocket? Real actual money? Who hasn't had that dream?? Eleanor has absolutely had that dream. Sam has absolutely had that dream. There are so many reasons to think about California, but who among us ever really does? America was supposed to be a dream, and also a promise, but what wasn't? Sam promised Eleanor he'd save $2,000 and Eleanor dreams of their life together like some movie where everybody wins. I've told you about those dreams before. A porch upstairs and a porch downstairs. A garage. What I mean is, have you ever thought about trying to build the rest of your life in a series of rent-stabilized apartments? The moment you outgrow one you have to find another, and they always rise to meet the market, which hangs above you like a noose. Every year of your life will cost more than the last, and then you'll die, and whoever is still alive that you loved will be gifted your debt. Anyway, a house is the kind of dream you dream in fall. Yes the leaves are dead, but can you remember when they were alive? Come over to my house. Please, just come over. Dinner's ready. I left the light on since it gets dark so early. It's been years and years and I have missed you so very much.

Even astronauts can understand something like this.

OK so it's 1980. The President declares a nationwide moratorium on towns burning to the ground. For one thing, there's a fuel shortage. For another, it's a pretty tired metaphor for change. For another, the whole notion that change has to be this violent, cathartic act . . . It's troubling. To say that pain is the one thing that can redeem us? It's short-sighted, and it's cruel. Love, said the President, once, is the truest revolution there is. To say that it'll split you open and make you anew is to not understand how your bones knit a home for your heart, which beats so brightly in that chest of yours, the one that just falls away, as we all melt into light. The President weeps, and the nation weeps with him. And then in 1981, the President, in his second act as President, declares the last President to be a township, and a witch, before burning the last President to the ground. Rules, declares the President, are for the poor, and the weak. How do you expect to reach that shining city on the hill? It is to be made of gold. And all around it will burn, so that its glory may be multiplied a thousandfold.

Listen, whoever decided to call it *welfare* was absolutely on to something. It's amazing to hear everyone railing against welfare, about how evil it is, when the fucking word means the health, happiness, and good fortune of a group. It's an anti-poverty program. The only reason you don't want a social safety net is because you want everyone who has less than you to starve and die, and it's interesting that, after the Voting

Rights Act passed and America finally became a democracy
in 1965 (I'm kidding, I know we're not a democracy, we're
barely a democratic republic, think about how much more of
a say corporations have than people), the depiction of people
on welfare went from poor whites to poor blacks and soon
after this welfare became evil, but I guess that's between you
and your God. In Heaven, today, the angels are restless. I
mean, they're always restless, but today it's to such a degree
that I found it worth noting.

OK so its 1989. We're in a seaside town. That's all I can tell
you for sure. Whatever happened in 1989 in this seaside town
is lost to history, which is written by the victors, who own all
the vacation properties, which they will happily rent to you at
a fair price set by the market. You deserve a vacation. You got
a job, you got married, you started a family, but there were
some complications during the birth, everything was fine!, the
baby's healthy and so's the mom!, but since hospitals should
be able to make money too, it's only fair, you don't want the
hospital's kids to go hungry, to have to go to community college, well, the bill set you back a bit, but then you worked your
ass off, and everything turned out great in the long run!, but
now you hardly see those kids you fought so hard to provide
for, and wouldn't you just love a week or two at the beach?
Playing catch all day, sipping a drink so cold your teeth want
to die, but they don't, getting drunk with the love of your life
as the sun sets, the kids so tired out they go straight to bed,
everyone glowing?

I want you to think back to when you were thirteen, four-teen, you found yourself in the living room, at home, your parents' home because you're thirteen, fourteen, and you live with them, and you don't know how you got there. Earlier you were in your bedroom, and now you're in the living room. Nothing exists between those two facts. The world just elided itself. That's what's happening now. We are very much in love, and have never been scared of money, or loneliness.

Do you see what I'm talking about?

Close your eyes.

Listen close.

Can you see it?

In the distance?

THE MOON STARTS TO GLOW, low in the sky. When I say *glow*, I mean the moon looks like those lights they use while digging up highways. I mean the moon is a lamp. I mean it's burning. I mean it's so bright you can't see a thing. The grass dies, the meadow chokes, the trees drop their leaves to the ground, where they, too, burn. The moon turns its back. In the morning everything is different. In the morning this'll be a sound investment, it'll be a traffic jam, it'll be a one-room shack at the edge of the world while the sky falls, it'll be the last home you'll ever dream of, it'll be just like that, it'll be different, and new, and it'll hold you, for the rest of your life, as the tanks roll in. But it's not morning yet. That's later. This is now. And now, there's just fallow fields and skeleton trees as far as the eye can see. Good night. Sleep tight. I'll see you in the morning. I love you so very, very much.

I know you've been waiting for the tanks to roll in, but the tanks already rolled in, they rolled in in Ferguson, in 2016, as police rode them down the street to murder anyone who was upset that they were murdering people. I mean the tanks have been here the whole time. Why do you think busses have such trouble getting up Classon?

Also, did you know that *glitch* is a Yiddish word?

Their lease was coming up for renewal soon, and Sam and Eleanor absolutely were going to pay whatever it said because

there was no way in hell that they were going to pack up everything they have ever bought in their whole entire lives and then
packed into this two-bedroom in Crown Heights that would
probably definitely be pitched as being in Prospect Heights so
as to rise to meet the market which hangs over us all like a
noose, and it's the little things, like there's a garbage room
with a chute, and the maintenance guys are all nice with incredibly sad eyes, and they all have the same name in that there
is one name and whoever is holding the phone that you call to
say you need something, that's Bruce today. Not one of these
men is named Bruce. They're shaped one way or the other way,
they have nimble fingers no matter what you think, they can
do pretty much everything, you give them a few bucks because
you have no idea what they're paid and they came by at 11:45
at night because you both locked your keys and it only cost
forty bucks for them to drill the lock and give you a new key
for the new lock and when things are made easier for you it's
always easier to say yes. Dear God it feels good to say yes to
things! To say yes, yes, yes, yes, yes, yes, yes, yes, yes, yes yes
yes yes yes yes yes yes! Try it. I dare you. One day Sam and
Eleanor are going to say yes and it's going to be incredible. It
could happen any day. Any day! I swear to God!

Above us, far far above us, is the International Space Station.
Not even the secret police can get there. Everyone pisses in
bags and looks at the moon. It seems incredible. We're all too
old to become astronauts. We would have needed to train our
whole lives for this one purpose. Can you imagine that? Eleanor absolutely thinks about this all the time. This and being

a ballerina. Haven't you ever wanted to be a ballerina? Jesus
Christ just imagine being able to have that level of discipline
over anything at all, let alone your own body. It's too late for
Eleanor to be a ballerina. But, I gotta ask!, is it too late for
the unhoused?, for the people being shoved in the cop car?,
for your rent to stop going up faster than your income does?
It might be too late for health care, or the collective student
loan debt (which is sitting at around $1,700,000,000,000) or
to fix the pipes in Flint. It would cost, according to estimates,
around $200,000,000 to fix the pipes in Flint. And who has
that kind of money? Eleanor and Sam don't. Americans spending $3,800,000,000,000 a year on health care don't. The busi-
nesses going out of business because they can't compete with
two-day shipping don't. Sure Jeff Bezos makes too much in a
second to even say out loud because it'll be that much higher
next time you check (seriously though go check, right now, I'll
wait), and Bill Gates has $129,500,000,000, and if you want
there's a fun website where you can spend his money on all
kinds of things! But what nobody seems to account for is that
nobody really gives a fuck if any of us live or die! Because if
they did, then we'd all have health insurance, and jobs, and
more than enough money for food, and for housing. Every
single American. And we don't. So we have to assume it's
because nobody gives a fuck. There is only one thing in this
world that it is never, ever too late for. It is never, ever too late
to love with an open heart.

A hospital stay in the US costs about $5,220 per day and in,
say, Australia it costs $765.

Sam had a headache. He was laying down. That's all from
Sam. Sam wondered if the secret police could blackbag this
headache. Solidarity means get them the fuck out of your
thoughts, Sam, aside from the knowledge that they could, at
any moment, blackbag you into a van, never to be seen again.
One day your whole life will be tossed into a black bag that
gets tossed into a van and driven to a place you'll never be
seen from again and the light, Jesus, a black bag, please, it's
too bright, it's too loud, and his right eye is going to explode,
there is just such a fucking pressure around it. In the living room is Eleanor, reading, hoping Sam is OK, knowing
there's nothing she can do, that if she asks she has to go in,
quiet, and whisper, *Baby what can I do?* and Sam'll ask for a
hot washcloth, and silence, and a bowl for the cloth, it only
works for one minute, then it's not hot anymore, this is the
one thing a microwave would be good for but neither of them
trust microwaves, which are only good for reheating take-
out and keeping hot damp washcloths hot and damp. There
are no miracles left on Earth we haven't built and yes, there
are times when that gives me pause. Eleanor wonders how
much of this sort of non-miraculous thinking is because she
hasn't gone into the office in almost two months because her
coworkers refuse to get flu shoots because the flu shots are
full of chips and those chips will be used to track them and
they tell her this from their phones which are connected to
their watches that monitor their biological data and send it
up into the cloud, if it's because she isn't leaving her desk to
walk through Union Square Park every two hours, and Eleanor thinks about how she isn't going out much at all, I mean

anywhere, and that recently the world feels like it's shrinking around her. When you start thinking the world has no more miracles left, you should probably take a walk. Eleanor goes to whisper in Sam's ear that she's going to take a walk in the park. It's a beautiful day. She leaves a fistful of Excedrin beside him, and the coldest water she can find. Eleanor walks to the park. Sam drinks a bucket of water. The trees look alive. It's hard to think about the waving yellow and red as being on fire when you think about the parts of the country that are, currently, on fire, like, say, the Cuyahoga River, the states of Washington and Oregon and California where the sky is red, I mean red, and the smoke is so thick you can chew it, but you can't breathe it, you can't breathe the air, and the borders are either closed or closing, nobody really seems to know, I'm sorry. Sam is sitting in the shower, the water as hot as he can get it to be, with a washcloth over his face, and the lights off. The police are loading bodies out of buildings and into trucks. The bodies are already in black bags. They just drag the bag with the body out the building and then, as a team, toss them into the trucks, which are double-parked on every street, so, good luck. Everybody in New York dreamed about death that month. Later, they dreamed about something else. Eleanor is watching the sun move over the leaves. She is very glad Sam talked her into prescription sunglasses, which she thought would be a stupid expense, since they don't drive, since they live in Brooklyn, so why would she need to see with sunglasses? And Sam would say, *for that*, and point to the sun moving over the trees, and he was right. She took them off. She put them on.

Eleanor tells Sam that there's something wrong with the toilet, because there is. "Text Bruce, Sam." It is Sam's job to text Bruce and tell whoever is currently holding the phone that there is something wrong, and then a man named Bruce appears at the door any time between one hour and six weeks after the text. You can call Bruce but since you never know which Bruce is holding the phone texts are easier because there's a record of the text. Bruce appears. Today Bruce is from Ecuador and he installs a new toilet seat while telling them how much he misses the sky. No longer do they start sliding to one side while shitting! Stability is here for all! They tip Bruce. Tomorrow Bruce is an entirely round man with the saddest eyes you've ever seen and he lives with his wife and their daughter and his granddaughters in the basement, where all Bruces live. Apparently it's going to be cold tonight. Thank God we have each other.

OK so the forty-hour week. "Eight hours for work, eight hours for rest, eight hours for what we will." That was what they chanted while they were being killed in the streets. So, technically, you work eight hours a day, with an hour for lunch, but that hour doesn't count towards the eight, so let's say nine hours of your day are spent at work, and something like thirty to forty-five minutes for your commute each way each day, let's just call it an hour and a half, so that's now ten and a half hours of the day devoted to work, leaving you with thirteen and a half hours of the day that belong to you, and you really need to sleep for at least six of them, if not eight, so that's like what, five and a half to seven and a half hours of the day that are yours? Plus the weekend? Again, people died for this level of freedom. People were willing to die to win you basically six hours that are yours Monday through Friday, and the weekend. They died for that. I really need you to understand that killers were hired to try to prevent workers from winning this. What have we done with their deaths? What have we done with the lives they put on the line so ours would have a bit more freedom? The only thing to do is be willing to die for a thirty-six-hour workweek. I honestly don't see how this happens, but it's a beautiful thought. We all just owe so much now. I am absolutely willing to die so that no one has to live like this ever again. Is how we live really so bad? I don't know! But why is it you can only want more if you have more than enough? Why is that if you have less than what you need, you can't ever ask for more, and if you have more than what you need, they just give it to you? I know, I know, that that's how capitalism works, that that's its purpose, to keep a loose caste system of workers and own-ers and middle management who will never be owners and so they have to be grateful to not be workers, but it's always just the people who work and the people who pay them, and we could, you had better fucking believe it, get whatever we wanted, if we could all just agree on what we wanted, and not work again till we got it. Fred Hampton knew this, and he knew what to do about it, and you had better absolutely believe that that is why the greatest coalition builder the left has ever known has been dead in his bed since December 4, 1969, and if any of us figure out how to successfully agitate for a thirty-six-hour workweek you had better believe we'll be shot in the fucking face by fucking cops in our fucking beds while we fucking sleep, and I gotta ask you, would it be worth it to die if you knew the world would end up better than it was before? And then I gotta ask you, is it worth it to the world to lose you if you're willing to do that? To lose someone that committed to the fight?

This would all be a lot funnier if there wasn't all this blood on our hands!

OK so it's January 22, 1919, and the Red Summer has just begun! Summer at the end of January, who'd have thought! The Red Summer began with lynchings and its early stages peaked on July 3 when the police in Bisbee, Arizona decided to murder the US Tenth Cavalry, more commonly known as the Buffalo Soldiers. In late July, in Chicago, the FBI filed worried reports that leftists were winning converts in the black community and, fifty years later, they killed Fred Hampton, because it turns out that pointing out that the cops and the state want you dead for wanting a better life is kind of effective, and then September brought the formation of the African Blood Brotherhood, an armed resistance that took to the streets to protect their communities from the violence of the state. In November, the National Equal Rights League wrote the President, begging him to do to his country what he forced Poland and Austria to do by going to war with them, and to address and right the horrific treatment of America's racial minorities. The President did not. The Red Summer lasted from January 22 to December 27 or November 13, depending on your sources. It's the same story over and over again and it's exhausting. I'm tired. The Tulsa Massacre was in 1921 and at least three hundred black Americans were killed in those two days. It is estimated that 250 black Americans were killed during the Red Summer. Last year 1,126 people were killed by the police in America and the year before that it was 1,095 and the year before that it 1,144 and the year before that it was 1,089, it's estimated that 5,800 homeless people died on the streets but it's really fucking hard to get an accurate number of a transient population we actively try to destroy, and about seventy-two million Americans have some form of medical debt and around 45 million Americans have student loan debt and about 120 million Americans have credit card debt, but soon it'll be Diwali and then it'll be Thanksgiving and then it'll be Hanukkah and then it'll be Christmas, and there will be snow on the ground, and lights in the windows, and the world will be full of joy, it will be spilling out of everything, like light, until it is all we can see. So just you wait. I'm sure if we all just sit patiently and wait, the world will fill with light, and the kingdom of Heaven will redeem us all.

So, since we're talking about reckonings, and that which we can never atone for, this is a great time to talk about angels!

In the Bible we learn that God's presence, even God's voice, is so beyond our understanding that to bare any sort of witness to it would result in our absolute destruction for (as God told Moses in Exodus 33:20, loosely translated "you cannot see my face and live," but I'm not a translator, and I know a

lot of good work has been done about translating the Bible
and the genuine mistakes that have been made, and anyway
the point is that) God is beyond us. Angels were represented
to us as balls of light, covered in wings and eyes, fracturing
off into dimensions we could never understand. So that's an
angel. Angels are also portrayed as absolutely naked babies
with small cute wings and scrolls floating always and perfectly over their sex. Angels have been shown as sad people in
overcoats with wings that float in and out of existence, they
have been shown in gilded armor and with fiery swords, their
wings spread wide, blotting out the sun. At what point did
we decide angels should be something we could understand,
when the Bible clearly states that the war in Heaven was
because God made us so different, and so capable of independence? Why is it that they went from utterly unknowable
to perfect versions of us, hot as shit, gilded to the tits, with
enormous wings, and the fiery sword of God's most divine
judgment? Anyway it's worth thinking about, the things that
exist that we could never understand, the ways in which we
stretch ourselves ragged and thin to explain the world, to
make this all somewhat easier to bear, to find new and wondrous ways to live lives devoid of mystery, and untouched by
the divine.

Sam cannot stop thinking about this while playing the
game where the angels, finally, come. They come in so many
ways! They come at Christmas, blocking out the sun, the
land covered in snow, the snow a kind of ash, our futures
lost in a fire, they come as a wind in the door, as a swiftly
tilting planet, hidden by the moon until too late, they come

at night, in the day, they come for the banks, they sit in final and eternal judgment of the men and the women who set themselves up as the cullers of the flock of the race we call man, the angels come in judgment, they come in love, they stop a bus, they remove the black bags from the secret police, they can't be everywhere when this happens, when you try to save people you can only ever save one at a time in the game, you can try to figure out the best person to save but when you do that you only ever end up saving one person, you want to save as many people as you can you have to just save people, and whatever they go on to do with their lives hangs over what passes for an angel's soul for the rest of their lives, which are endless, and eternal, like the dawn. The judgment of angels is final, and their deliberations are a mystery. We're all doing our best here. Is Sam thinking about Eleanor's body? You absolutely know he is. Meanwhile, off in the distance of America, a police precinct is on fire. On the street, in front of the flames licking the very sky clean, is painted the sentence DO YOU HEAR US NOW?

HELLO, said the news, IT IS TIME FOR THE YEAR IN REVIEW! THIS YEAR WE LEARNED SO MUCH, AS A NATION. IT WAS THE YEAR AMERICA SAID "HELLO I HAVE MISSED YOU!" TO RACE RIOTS, IT WAS THE YEAR SAM LEARNED HOW TO SAVE MONEY, IT WAS THE YEAR EVERYBODY WEPT SO MUCH THAT WE STARTED REPORTING ON ALL THE WEEPING, THE YEAR ISN'T EVEN OVER, said the news. ISN'T IT AMAZING THAT WE'RE DOING THIS YEAR-END REVIEW NOW, IN WHATEVER MONTH

IT IS? ANYWAY IT WAS THE YEAR A CLOUD LIVED IN PROSPECT PARK FOR A MONTH, IT WAS THE YEAR THE ANGELS CAME, said the news, OR WAS IT???? I'M JUST KIDDING, IT WAS THE YEAR OF THE DRIVE-IN MOVIE, THE YEAR OF PEOPLE RENTING CARS JUST TO DRIVE IN TO THE MOVIE, TO SIT IN THE CAR AND WATCH IT ALL, TO FEEL, FINALLY, FREE, FOR THE FIRST TIME SINCE CHILDHOOD.

It's starting.

Shh.

"SAM," SAID ELEANOR, in the middle of the night, "have you noticed that the world keeps getting stranger?" "Yes," said Sam. Sam got up and got them both the coldest water the taps had to offer. Eleanor went to the bathroom. She came back to bed, where she found Sam, and a cold glass of water. She curled up in his arms. "I love you so much, Sam." Sam brushed her hair with his hand, rested it on her cheek, and kissed her head. "You are the light of my fucking life," he said, "and I love you with all my heart." Meanwhile, people kept dying.

At one hundred thousand people blackbagged, they listed every name on the front page. At two hundred thousand blackbagged, it was a brief article below the fold, and at five hundred thousand blackbagged it really didn't merit a mention anymore, there were some other things to talk about, they were pretty important. At six hundred thousand blackbagged they blackbagged the paper, just to be safe. Eleanor went out and picked up a rotisserie chicken sandwich on a crusty potato roll swiped with aioli and a sort of onion-radish slaw. She ate this at home, at her desk, where she was working. She checked her email. A dog was barking. Did the neighbors have a dog? It sounded familiar, the dog, barking. She went to go look for the dog. She was in the office. How did she get in the office? Eleanor pinched herself. "What are you doing there, princess?" asked her boss. Her boss called all women princess. Eleanor had always assumed it was because none of them had any actual power and this was a hollow title meant to make them feel special. "Dream check," said Eleanor, qui-

etly, maybe wishing she hadn't. This was probably real. Eleanor wanted to ask Sam if she was at home or at work, like if
her body was in two places, but Sam, she remembered, was
also at work, and would have left before her anyway. Sam
couldn't help. *Am I at home, or at work?* she texted him. *send
pics*, texted Sam, and she did. Sam said, *this would appear
to be your office, darlin*, and Eleanor said, *I was getting a
sandwich at The Fly and now I'm at work wtf*, and Sam said,
that is a long walk you hate walking, and she said, *Walking
sucks, Sam, it's too much work*, and Sam said, *maybe you're
in two places at once and when you get home you'll be in
one place, there'll just be the one of you.* Her sandwich is at
her desk, in the office, where she works. Eleanor picks up the
sandwich and wanders around the office. This is absolutely
the sandwich she bought from The Fly just blocks from their
apartment and it's definitely still warm. Does The Fly serve
lunch? There are dogs barking. More than one now. This is
what made her realize she was in the office. Eleanor starts
to follow the sound of the dogs. Eleanor wishes Sam was at
home to check on things, but Sam's at work. Eleanor's, apparently, also at work. These are the facts. Eleanor can't call
home because they don't have a landline. Eleanor calls herself
but she's busy. That's typical. Eleanor texts Sam, *It'd be fun
to get like an amber alert for the end of the world*, and Sam
dies laughing. Sam gets resurrected at his desk, immediately,
where he sits and does several things on the computer which
he needs a second monitor to accomplish. He meets Eleanor
at Prospect Park. It's the end of the day and nobody knows
how they got there. Eleanor hears dogs bark, but of course she
does, it's the park. They stare at the leaves on the trees as they

finally fall. At home, in bed, Sam asks Eleanor, "Did you ever figure out about today?" and Eleanor says to Sam, "Life is a mystery, Sam," and Sam says, "Boy howdy," and holds her close all through the night.

It was getting colder every day! You couldn't even sleep with the windows open anymore!

Sam walks in one door and out another. One door opens to a forest, one door opens to the kingdom of Heaven, I'm just kidding, the kingdom of Heaven is within us all!, get a grip!, one door opens to the rest of your life, one door opens to the Presidency or some other office involving an appointment, one opens to the future, which is bright and shining, and the other opens on a thunderstorm, there are two doors, is what I'm saying, and at the end of each day, Sam has to open one door, and then another, to come home.

You don't need to learn how to bake an incredible sourdough if you can buy one. I'm sorry, I know self-sufficiency is incredible, but if someone else can do something better than you can, it's OK to let them! These are things Eleanor thinks regularly. Geronimo has been baking bread all fall. His focaccia is really good. Sam goes over for focaccia and brings some wine. They just sit there listening to whatever Chet Baker album Geronimo found on the internet. It's a really nice night. Eleanor calls her mom. Eleanor's mom has tweaked her neck

again. The pain run downs her shoulder, beneath her shoulder blade, the nerves beneath her armpit are pinched, calling
on the phone sucks, it's the one joy of the way phones have
headphones with microphones that basically always work, is
that you can just talk when you're in pain once you find the
spot on the floor that makes this all a bit easier. This is what
throw pillows are for, for arranging on the ground so you
can call your daughter without your whole life becoming one
dull constant all-consuming ache. "Are you guys doing Hanukkah this year?" her mom asks, and they are, because Sam
bought them a beautiful menorah this summer, on sale even.
Later, her mom tells her a story. Her mom says, "When you
were a little girl, there was this storm," "It was an enormous
storm, mom," "I know that part. That's the only part I know.
Will you tell me the rest? I'm tired, and I'm sore. Please?" So
she did.

Meanwhile!

Geronimo sits in his office during office hours to help the students to get their papers to read like something other than
a series of paragraphs lifted from the internet and stitched
together with fonts and margins. A student sits across from
Geronimo. Geronimo did not hear him come in, and looks up,
startled. Geronimo's glasses fall off his face and hang from
the cord around his neck. His suit is beautiful, and rumpled,
and a sort of faded olive, with a soft cream-and-lilac color-
blocked shirt. The student has shaved his head. While I was

telling you what Geronimo was wearing, the student, who is sitting across from Geronimo, was shaving his own head. He could be in sweatpants or a tuxedo. It doesn't really make a difference, and either way, the student wants Geronimo to tutor him over the summer. Geronimo tells the student he doesn't really do that, and the student says, "My parents will pay you," and Geronimo asks how much, and the student calls his parents, who tell him exactly how much. If I told you it was enough, I would not be telling you enough. The student's apartment overlooks the Hudson. Geronimo's whole apartment could fit in the living room, which has a grand piano and a basketball hoop, the kind where the base is full of sand to weight it down. On the edge of the living room is a screen door to a patio. There's a hall closet you could rent to children and stack them five high. There's a hall closet rented to children, they're stacked five high. The student corners Geronimo. The student had a problem with substances. The student has a problem with poetry. The parents, concerned, call, for the bill is at their feet, and it has come due. It is not made clear to Geronimo which bill they are referring to. He tries to leave but it turns out that's not possible. He contacts a lawyer, but they're a bit tied up at the moment. The student writes a paper on knots. The student's a bit tied up. Geronimo hasn't thought about Isabella once. Geronimo hangs by a thread, or a ledge. Geronimo's life takes on the scope of *Die Hard*, but in an apartment. The Germans are played by the student. Bruce Willis is played by the President. Geronimo slips out the back. In the mail, there's a check. It's an incredible check. He truly cannot believe it. He shows it to Sam, who immediately dies. Sam's ghost returns to his body. "Wow," says Sam. Eleanor calls Geronimo. "Did you just kill my Sam?" she asks and Sam, whose ghost has just returned to his body, declares himself to be fine, and Geronimo, confused, orders him and Sam some more drinks.

Isabella woke up and her husband was a bird. He told her he was a ghost. Her dreams make more sense this way. Time makes more sense this way. Tense is a lie because our memories are just stories we tell ourselves as they're happening. The bird flies away. "Fuck you!" she shouted. She shouted "FUCK YOU!!!" until there's no more air in her lungs, in the castle, in all of Italy, and that bird falls dead. Then Isabella burned the castle to the ground. She went to sleep on the grass. The whole world smelled like a campfire. Her love was a ghost story she could forget if she tried and she did. She didn't dream of anything at all. It was incredible.

In the morning, the castle was back and so were her memories, and the whole wide world. On the radio a man sang about how when a heart breaks it makes a beautiful sound. Isabella sets the radio on fire, and the song is never heard again.

The President is alone, the President is with others, the President is bombing children, the President is bombing children alone, with others, this is boring, what I mean is that this is what Presidents do, all of them, and it's what they will probably always do, and we'd all be better off if we knew about it, and I really wish we could talk about something else, because it's exhausting, which is why we can't! We can't always look away when we want to talk about something else! And also, yknow, sometimes you do. Sometimes you have to make dinner, and you check your bank account, and there is somehow more than you thought because you've managed to get a very very small handle on your debt because you're working, because this is what it's like to have stability, and it's insane that this isn't enough, that none of this could ever be enough, and here we all are, with our aching bodies, and our hearts bursting with love, just desperately wanting to not have to worry about food and shelter, and why the fuck isn't the internet a public utility when absolutely everyone needs it to work, to live, and Fred Hampton is still dead. Sam is cooking pork chops for dinner tonight. They're going to be delicious.

In the park someone built a cross or a temple, they built it out of the park, out of the grills and the trees, the goats who graze, the beer cans, they built it to last as long as the rest of us, which, depending on your source, is either an awful short time or an awful medium time, they built it to float, they built it to sink, to worship, they built it to save them, to be saved, one day, by something so far beyond them as to defy explanation. Sam ordered a pizza and a mountain of Lactaid. They could, finally, have it all. Eleanor looked at the plants in the apartment with love. When all this is underwater, they will never, ever go thirsty. When the clouds die and the sun blankets this land they will never be lonely. Outside, the trees shudder and shake in the wind. The secret police have taken all the balconies in the city. Geronimo is on the ground, he's homeward bound, he fell asleep on the subway and it worked out fine anyway, he is walking across the bridge from South Ferry, he's doing his best. In his bedroom is a bird. You know exactly which bird I'm talking about. "Get the fuck out of here," says Geronimo. "I can't ever go back there," says the bird. "(Gasp)," gasps Geronimo. *Sam*, writes Geronimo, *How many shots at the miraculous do we really get in this life?*

I do not always know how to keep my heart open.

Geronimo's on a plane across the water. The Cuyahoga's still on fire and Berlin's skies are forever gray. The secret police are in your dreams and that's why you keep forgetting about them. They throw their black bags into vans and drive the vans into the sea, which is a river, and one day it will swallow us all. This is stolen land. You forget that at your own peril. Once upon a time it was summer. Sam and Eleanor were at summer camp, and they were children, and then there was a storm. Everyone ran around trying to do their best and then they got swallowed by the lake, which rose up like a great wave. Sam and Eleanor ended up in a tree. After this they wouldn't see each other again for years until Sam walked into a party one night and a light came on and there was Eleanor, bathed in light. Back at summer camp, they were all that was left. They did everything they could to build a life, to build a warmth, to give each other something to live for. They never kissed, they were absolutely terrified to kiss, they held each other all night, they told each other stories about the future, about the world to come, and then, one day,

it came.

NOW IT'S THE FUTURE, which is today. The snow is slowly starting, once more, to fall. Sam and Eleanor light the last candle on the menorah. They've done the smallest presents this year. Next year they'll do big presents at Hanukkah and little presents at Christmas. Tomorrow they'll buy the tree. It's tomorrow. They buy the tree. It's huge. It's taller than Sam. It's not that hard, he's barely six feet, but it's seven feet, which is absolutely tall, and it's absolutely great that Sam got a step ladder when he lived with Geronimo, who was tall enough to change the lightbulbs without it, but Sam was not, and spent one weekend shitting in total darkness because of this. Sam and Eleanor are trimming the tree. They're wrapping the enormous white bulbs around it, and they're making the same mistake they always make where they put the layers too close together, realize they're gonna run out halfway through, and readjust worriedly and hurriedly as they go, with a movie about the spirit of Christmas on the TV, the spirit of Christmas is, I think, about giving, about giving of yourself to others, and the absolute warmth this can bring us at the time of year when we see the sun for less than six hours, and we need to find anything we can to keep warm. Geronimo is in Italy. The Cuyahoga has frozen over. The city of Cleveland rejoices. The snow falls and falls. Sam and Eleanor hang the red balls. They put the cardboard star on top of the tree. They put the presents under the tree. They get into bed. The streetlights are on. They keep getting brighter. The room begins to fill with light. The whole world begins to fill with light. There is nothing between us, between any of us, there is nothing but light. Sam says to Eleanor, "I love you," and it comes out as light and Eleanor says to Sam, "I love you," and it comes out as nothing but light, I love you, I love you, I love you, I love you, I love you, I love you, I love you, I love you, I love you, I love you, I love you, I love you

This is when the angels come.

ACKNOWLEDGMENTS

Thank you to Wikipedia, the encyclopedia of the people; thank you to every journal that published parts of this book over the last few years: shitwonder, Blush, Triangle House Review, and The Baffler; thank you to Rob Ozga for the help with baseball research; thank you to Gerry Coletta, presidential expert; thank you to J. W. McCormack for championing my work and for helping me make this book a stronger book; thank you to my parents for reading every single thing I write and for nurturing me as an artist and a person; thank you to twitter for breaking my brain; thank you to baseball for filling my heart with joy and spite; thank you to Josef Kaplan, with love and solidarity; thank you to Michelle Lynn King for being a champion and a pal; thank you to Hilary Leichter for being one of the best readers I could ever ask for; thank you to Alex Kleeman and Amelia Gray and Blake Butler for over a decade of friendship and support, I owe you all so much; thank you to Kip Adams and Jay Deshpande and Josh and Nalini Edwin for your friendship in the rough years of the early drafts of this, and to David Burr Gerard, Bryan Woods, and Liam Powell for your friendship as I wrapped it up; thank you to Monika Woods for believing in me and this book; thank you to Athena Bryan for the way you have understood this story and shepherded it out into this wild fucking world; and thank you to Peter Kranitz, Beste Miray Doğan, and the Melville House production team for their incredible work on this; and, ultimately, thank you to Alexandra Tanner, the light of my life, for the love you have shown me, for the kind wonder you have brought into my life, and for every single thing you did to make this a better book than I knew how to make it. I love you.